He drew his pistol and waited. In the distance, he heard what sounded like the chilling, woman-like scream of a panther. He wondered if the powerful, feline creature had been sneaking through the forest . . . following him.

When the cry came again, the chill in him mounted. He realized it wasn't the sound of a panther. . . . It was the cry of a woman. He dismounted, and with a drawn pistol, edged along the grass. Then suddenly, he saw a halted carriage. As he stepped closer, the screams grew louder, and he could hear the sound of struggling.

Inside, a man was trying to attack a woman.

Tightening his grip on his pistol, Jake eased closer to the carriage. A storm of outraged thoughts streaked through his mind. But even as the images swirled into his brain, he lunged forward and wrenched open the nearest door . . .

RIDE
TO
REVENGE

BY ERIC ALLEN

ZEBRA BOOKS
KENSINGTON PUBLISHING CORP.

ZEBRA BOOKS

are published by

KENSINGTON PUBLISHING CORP.
21 East 40th Street
New York, N.Y. 10016

First Printing: November, 1979

Printed in the United States of America

CHAPTER ONE

The U.S. deputy marshals tried to halt him when his big horse thundered off the western end of Fort Smith's new Jay Gould Bridge that summer of 1894. But his mount was much too fast for them as he reined across the tip of the earth-filled levee that edged the Arkansas River shore. He continued westward, almost certain that none of the marshals would puncture his spine with long-range rifle shots. He didn't figure they were the kind of lawmen who would shoot even a notorious gunman in the back.

A tall, gaunt Cherokee and his wife, cutting pokeweeds near the levee, saw his horse coming. They scurried aside, and the Indian shielded his eyes against the westering sun. "Jake Spaniard! That son-buck's killed 'nother man somewhar, Conchie! Reckon it was close up right 'round here?"

"Naw. See them marshal men yonder? Guess what-all happened took place 'cross the river, maybe in Whiskey Smith."

Spaniard's horse gained even more speed on Albert Pike Road, west of the "Little Juarez" town of Moffett—Indian Territory. In the whip of the wind, he had to hold down his hat. He used one hand for that chore and gripped the double-barreled shotgun with the other, while keeping proper tautness on the racing horse's reins.

He wondered, for a moment, if he should have taken the killer's shotgun and shells. But facing grimly into the wind, he decided he had used good judgment. After all, the killer's cronies might have grabbed them and downed him before he could have reached his horse and mounted on Fort Smith's Garrison Street.

He didn't slow the big horse he was riding, or even look back as water churned under him at the northern edge of Grassy Lake. Waves kicked up and spirals of muddy slough licked out like snakes' tongues on either side. Then there was the lift of the uplands, and he saw the Fort Smith-Muskogee stagecoach stopped on the halfway station grounds between the Indian Territory town of Muldrow and the border at Whiskey Smith. Old Dutch Cagle, driver of the coach, was waiting, just as he had promised.

Jake Spaniard tucked the butt of the shotgun under his right knee, pulled a jackknife from his trouser pocket and reached around and slit the throatlatch of the bridle to save time when he reached the stage and to set the big horse free. As he slowed the horse and circled the halted stage, he leaned down and uncinched the saddle too. He felt himself tumbling as the horse skidded to a stop, but he was ready to catch his fall. He hurled saddle, bridle, blanket and all against the huge logs on the stage station's western side, then murmured a heartfelt word of apology to the big horse as he lashed its rump with the palm of his hand and sent it racing on. Then as old Dutch Cagle grinned at him, he boarded the coach by a side door, thrust an arm out an open window and gave the wave to go.

The four-up hitch lunged into the traces. Spaniard took a seat. It wasn't until then that he noticed another passenger—a woman quietly watching him from her place on the left-hand side of the seat. She didn't show any surprise. She pushed back a strand of her golden hair and continued watching him.

At last she said, "You board a coach fast, Mister Spaniard."

He scowled at her. "How come you know my name?"

She leaned slightly toward him. "I make it my business to know when men on the scout are coming home. I happen to know you've been in Old Mexico for years, waiting until the uproar about your last wild shooting scrape here died down."

Spaniard didn't say anything. He took shotgun shells for the double-barrel from his pocket, and began to uncrimp edges of the ends and pry out wadding that held powder and lead. He carefully poured buckshot from every shell onto the leather seat of the stagecoach. Then he

7

began to press pieces of denim from the bottom of his trousers into the hulls over the powder. Time after time, he slit off pieces of his trousers, pressed them hard over the powder, then swiftly recrimped the shells.

"What are you doing with those shotgun shells, Mister Spaniard?"

"Wadding without bullets in them, so neither a man or horse could be killed by a charge," he said.

"But why?"

His glance cut sideward. "I don't want to kill anything. Maybe just knock some horses' fore-legs. That won't lame them for keeps . . . What's your name?"

"Sabina Mulvane."

"Related to old Brack Mulvane?"

She nodded. "I'm his wife."

He felt a rankling fury surge through him at even the mention of the Mulvane name, but why speak his rage to a woman? He loaded the double-barrel with two wadded shells, then turned to look back along the path they'd trav-eled. There, he saw five U.S. deputy marshals galloping up the rise, west of Grassy Lake. He hoped his horse had raced on somewhere out of sight so they wouldn't suspect he was aboard the stage. But a baggage stop at Muldrow sud-denly smashed that hope to pieces.

The marshals overtook the stage at the sta-tion, and though they slowed their mounts to a jog-trot and kept traveling westward, Spaniard saw them glance suspiciously toward the crack

8

in the curtain he had rapidly drawn.

"Get down under the seats, or between them," he ordered Sabina Mulvane.

"But why, Mister Spaniard?"

"Because I got out of Whiskey Smith without a warrent being served on me. I killed the man that murdered Pa . . . and those marshals are no one's fools. I figure they'll stop this stage at the crossing of Big Skin, ready to haul me out. Get down, I tell you! I'm going topside now."

"You going to fight marshals from up there?"

"No. I'll be back inside, but however I handle things, this coach may be riddled with lead. Stay down!"

She nodded, and his scarred boots and snipped trouser legs led the way as he opened the window on his side and crawled out. He had a seat beside the driver in less than a minute.

"When we talked at Fort Smith, I didn't know a woman would board at the last minute, Jake," old Dutch apologized.

"Don't worry about it . . . Those marshals know I'm aboard, don't they?"

"Yep. Could tell it by th' cast of their eyes."

"All right . . . Now look here. When they stop you, don't try to stall, unless you do your regular stint of pleading for lives of passengers. That'll give me time to leave the inside of the coach through the door opposite them and put a double-barreled shotgun on 'em."

"You aim to kill?"

"No. You know better. I might have to shoot forelegs out from under a horse or two and dump

9

some riders. Then, damnit, you use your whip and drive this stage."

"I'm a pretty good driver of a four-up, Jake."

"I know you are." Spaniard took out a money pouch, opened it and pressed a hundred dollar bill into the old man's hand.

"You don't have to do this, Jake," old Dutch said.

"I know . . . But a decent man pays the fiddler when he dances. You see?"

"I guess so . . . And Jake, when or *IF* you get back aboard after the ruckus, I'll run this rig over any dead or live thing that gets in my way. This damned Fort Smith-Muskogee stage line is going broke anyhow since the railroad-highway bridge was built."

Jake Spaniard merely dipped his head, then with the litheness of a lynx, he swung around and dropped back inside the stage.

In a swirl of dust at the crossing of Big Skin, he saw the marshals' horses spin around. When the coach reached the crossing, three of the marshals lifted hands to halt the stage. Watching closely through a window, Jake Spaniard thought, "Well, one thing's for certain. Parker and old Jacob Yoes rounded up the best ones to try to take me in."

He instantly recognized Paden Tolbert, Heck Thomas, Bat Masterson and the part-colored deputy, Baz Reeves.

While old Dutch Cagle talked, trying to stall them temporarily, Spaniard eased the cocked shotgun out the side door opposite the marshals.

10

He walked around the left-hand front wheel of the stagecoach and, with surprising suddenness, levelled down on them. He saw some of the bravest of the brave freeze in their saddles, all staring at him.

"Fellows, you aren't going to serve papers or take me, so you might as well ride back to Whiskey Smith."

"We have to take you, Spaniard," Heck Thomas said.

"I won't allow it. Pa's killer was a rotten scoundrel, unfit to live anyhow. Vengeance is my motto, but I did shoot him in self-defense. So I'm not going back to the western district court and let old Hanging Judge Parker sentence me to the rope ... That son of a bitch, after killing Pa, tried to shoot me too ... But a man of my reputation ... do you think I could make Parker's packed jury believe that?"

Bat Masterson moved to the left beyond the lead hitch. Abruptly, he jerked his pistol.

"Spaniard ... Jake, you're going back to Fort Smith with us."

Spaniard lowered the muzzle of the double-barrel slightly and squeezed the front trigger with its wadded shell. He shot straight at the right knee joint of Masterson's mount. The horse went down with the close impact of wadding, then came up, but Masterson fell aside. His gun discharged into the dust. All the marshals were, by then, drawing their pistols. But old Dutch Cagle cracked his long whip over the heads of the four-up hitch, and the stagecoach, with

11

the horses rearing, plunged forward. The iron-pointed tongue of the stage and the neck yoke struck Paden Tolbert's mount and sent both horse and rider in a floundering flurry squarely into a summer huckleberry patch.

Old Cagle made the crossing of Big Skin and was shortly far away. He peered around into a window of the coach and found that Jake Spaniard had gotten back inside. Old Cagle smiled and cracked his whip again in sheer exuberance. "By God, I've got the fastest gunslinger on the middle border with me, and we're hellbent t'wards the west!"

Ahead was the old town of Hanson Wells.

CHAPTER TWO

But darkness had already settled in when the stagecoach reached the town. Jake remembered Hanson from Pa's moonshine-making and rustler days, but the community wasn't the same. Once the community had boasted a store, sawmill, gristmill, a hotel for Iron Mountain railroad workers and a scattering of horse lots where auction sales were held every Saturday night. Now the huddle of unpainted shacks looked ghostly under a crescent moon, plastered like a dirt dauber's nest in the heart of Indian Territory. Evidently, folks had moved out to the Sequoyah district courthouse town of Sallisaw, or back to Whiskey Smith.

He heard Sabina Mulvane following him as he left the stage and went to shake hands with old Dutch Cagle.

"A hell of a drive, Dutch. Thanks."

"Told you I could do 'er, man!" Cagle declared with pride.

"You bet. I'll grab a fast drink, Dutch, then try to rent a livery horse and get home to Ma and Lige. Been three years, you know."

"What was it like, ridin' in Mexico?"

"A son-of-a-bitching time! Mexican people are salt of the earth. And no marshals were on my heels."

Sabina said urgently, "Why don't we get into that place across yonder and have ourselves some drinks?"

"That's my aim . . . See you, Dutch."

The light in the saloon was dim, but he could see that most of the tables were taken and the bar was crowded.

Not a whiskey jar or jug could be seen on shelves behind the bar. Money was passed to a couple of balding roughnecks who in turn placed the funds beside a trap door that led to a basement room.

Only lemonade and other soft drinks were in plain sight. That was what made it a blind tiger saloon.

Spaniard knew the trap door that led to the whiskey could be barred from the underside at the tap of a boot. When the revenuers came or when one was suspected, the whiskey could be toted swiftly through an underground tunnel to another hiding place. That was the way they did it when Pa's whiskey trade among the Indians was going strong.

He saw at a glance that there weren't many women there but that the place was packed with men: big, heavy-bodied, dark men in short sleeved shirts—city slickers, some of the back-woods people would have called them. Their presence here was strange to Spaniard, and a thought struck his mind: These men weren't cowboys, canal diggers or timber workers. They were a new breed he had never met.

He thought, "If I don't rent a horse, this may be a long-drawn night."

A man at a table whistled at Sabina Mulvane. He hesitated and half turned toward the man and recognized the rider. Resentment and rash-ness sped through Jake's veins. But he shrugged. It didn't mean anything. Sabina Mulvane meant nothing to him. The only thing he wanted from her was to find out how she had known he was coming home. Likely, she had warmed her way into friendship with his mother and his brother, Lige, and had found out from one of them.

A Cherokee girl and a fat white man sidled out to the floor to dance, but both were too drunk to keep time with the old player piano.

A young waitress dressed in a red ruffled skirt and neat blouse approached the table and stopped. She looked from Jake to Sabina, then swiftly back again.

"Two beers," Jake said, and the girl nodded, tossed back her loose brown hair and spun away. As she hurried past crowded tables, Jake Spaniard watched drunken men grab at her flow-ing skirt. This made him angry and he kept his eyes on her. She eluded every effort at stopping her as she went toward the bar where two heavy-

15

jowled barkeeps stood grinning. Such a pity that a pretty young girl like her has to work in a dive like this, Jake thought. But that had been the way of life in almost every region Jake had traveled, even as far away as Mexico.

Someone in the room whooped shrilly. When he turned to look out over the crowd, he saw the waitress weaving her way between the tables, carrying a tray with two mugs of beer and glasses. She was balancing the tray with one hand and smiling as she avoided pinching fingers. But he could see that she was tense and nervous. She threw her head up haughtily, and her free hand tossed back her loose brown hair. The gesture made him start probing his memory.

As the girl was nearing the booth, he suddenly remembered. That trim, spunky little waitress was Norma Clifton, Trudene's little sister! At first, he realized that Norma, the younger sister of the girl he was going to marry, would see him at a beer table with another woman and would misunderstand. She would tell Trudene what she thought she had seen. But he was just happy to see someone so close to Trudene . . . a member of the Clifton family right there before his eyes after three long years.

He braced his hands on the table. His lank form slid out of the booth as Norma neared, and when she set the beer down, he was fully upright.

"Norma!" he yelled.

Her eyes narrowed under long lashes. She took a swift step backward as if to avoid him. Then

16

recognition took hold and miraculously changed her expression.

She said incredulously, "My Lord! Jake Spaniard!"

Her laughter bubbled then, strong and happy. His long arms reached around her, holding her close for a moment. But then she freed herself and squirmed away as rapidly as she had approached. She looked at Jake, measuring the height and breadth of him, then glanced at Sabina Mulvane.

Sabina said mockingly, "An interesting little sideshow, but warm beer isn't much good. Ours is still waiting here, Mr. Spaniard."

Jake slid back into the booth. "Want to sit here with us awhile, Norma? Tell me about Trudene, and about yourself, you know?"

She said icily, "I don't think so. I have work to do . . . But I can tell you, my sister Trudene is all right."

Once again, she spun away and headed toward the bar, or to a table where someone had signaled her perhaps, Jake thought. He kept watching her.

"You seem disturbed, Jake," Sabina murmured. "Is it all that bad?"

He glared across at her. "When I want some comment from you, I'll ask."

"You think white slavery would fit her? . . . A girl like that, wearing a taunting and glaring red skirt?"

"Hell no! I guess she had to get a job somewhere. Her family never was well-off."

17

"That's too bad . . . that many people in this world are never very well-off."

Spaniard glared again, but didn't say anything. He sipped his beer and watched every move Norma Clifton made.

"My husband knows how to pick them, doesn't he?" Sabina Mulvane taunted with a laugh.

Spaniard drew his glance away from the waitress, frowning.

"What?" he snapped impatiently.

"You know what . . . That waitress in the beautiful red skirt," Sabina answered, smiling. "Brack starts the young and inexperienced here, then, as they learn their way around, they serve rather well in Brack's more plush places in larger middle-border settlements along the line of the Indian Nations . . . like places in Old Whiskey Smith, just over in Arkansas. You're bound to know what I mean."

"You're admitting to me that your husband owns this joint and many others, and trains young girls for a life of white slavery in addition to his smuggled whiskey trade?"

"Oh? . . . White slavery or smuggled whiskey? Did I mention such ugly words?"

"That's all this deal could be, if I know Brack Mulvane," Jake declared. "It's illegal to sell whiskey here in the Indian or Oklahoma Territories . . . at least in most of the Indian country, I've heard."

Sabina Mulvane shrugged. "Well, I suppose you do know Brack, in a way at least. You see, my husband has a way of making anything he

18

touches pay off . . . even some of the things that first went out but that he brought back not long after the Civil War."

"I have nothing except contempt for your husband. And Pa told me things about the Civil War that even Brack Mulvane never knew."

He ignored Sabina completely then, because trouble was about to break, and Norma was right in the middle of it with three grizzled drunks who were on their feet pestering her. Recalling Pa's war accounts, Jake considered strategy. He didn't think this was a time for hesitation. He eased from the booth, stepped around to the side of the man nearest him and hurled a looping sledgehammer right that caught the man just under the left ear and dropped him in his tracks. Spaniard moved up beside Norma then, seeing the near desperation in her eyes as she tried to free her left arm from another bearded man's tight grasp.

"Don't cause the little girl any trouble, friend," Jake commanded.

The man blinked once, then glanced down at the fellow Jake had floored. But the drunken man was too full of liquor to be impressed. He grinned and began to savagely twist Norma's arm.

"You think you're a privileged character?" he snarled at Jake. "You think you're the only one can flirt with a tavern girl like this?"

Spaniard knew at once he had made a bad mistake. He should have taken this snarly character out of the action fast, and first. Jake was in no position to hit the man flush, and he knew that a hard and flush blow would be the only kind that could count. Maybe a little parley would be best, Spaniard thought.

"I've never seen anything except bad trouble come out of a case like this," he said. "The little girl, here, she's had her share of trouble and aggravation tonight. I don't aim to see her have any more. She's done good service, I think, serving beer and all, trying to help everyone have a good time."

"Yah, helping YOU, maybe!" the bristling man cut in. "But not me! Why, me, I ain't had much of a good time at all. Not yit!"

He sucked in a deep breath, threw back his shaggy head and laughed, then abruptly quit it. His huge shoulders bunched, and one of his long arms swept out as if to encircle Norma's waist. Norma made a sort of whimpering sound, and Jake heard it plainly as he leaped closer. But she didn't cringe away from the man one whit. With one hand, she slapped him in the side of the face, then slammed him across the mouth with the other. For an instant Jake Spaniard halted, amazed at Norma's spunk as she crowded the astonished man backward, still slapping him.

Then, banging harshly above the racket in the room, Jake heard the opening and slamming of the front door. Through the quickness of the door's opening, he caught the faint glimmer of lantern light slanting against a sleek team of horses hitched to a new Spaulding hack. Then he recognized the man who had just come in. It was

Turk Munson, Brack Mulvane's stepson. Jake had hated Turk all his life, so the sight of him put him slightly off his guard. Sensing his distraction, the man on the right hit Jake with a blow that tore downward against his temple. Jake lashed back at the man, but missed. Then he lunged and caught Norma and pulled her away.

"Get out of this, Norma! Let me at that son-of-a-bitch!"

He went past her, seeing the fellow setting himself in a fighting stance.

For a time, the room had been comparatively quiet, but suddenly gang fight fear broke out with shouts and screaming and the sound of thrown and bursting bottles. Spaniard led with a powerful left hook that sent the fellow reeling sideward against a table. But even in that moment of stress, Jake could see Turk Munson's face out of the corner of his eye. It was this distraction that set the stage for catastrophe. When a rolling beer mug on the table met Jake's opponent's hand, he grabbed it and hurled it at Jake. He couldn't duck fast enough, and the hard, hammerlike bottom of the mug caught him in the chin. Chips of pain flaked off his jaw and splattered like shrapnel or canister shot against his brain. He dropped, and the man behind him kicked him in the side of the head. There was a short-lived dream before complete unconsciousness spread black muck across Jake Spaniard's mind.

CHAPTER THREE

During brief flashes of recurring conscious-
ness, he was aware of being carried somewhere.
He tried to struggle, but strong hands held his
arms and legs. Then something cold slammed
against his face, and he sat bolt upright, fully
awake. He was on a bed without a pillow. He
knew he had been stretched out flat on his back.
The room had sickly pink walls and a green
metal bedstead. He wondered briefly if he were
on a stopgap trip between heaven and hell. Then
he saw Sabina Mulvane, her pretty face calm,
composed. She was rubbing his forehead with a
cold damp cloth.

"Good boy! Big strong soldier! You're going
to be all right."

"Where am I?"

"In the old hotel near the saloon."

He pushed himself up further onto his elbows.
"Get me the hell out of here."

"Oh, not yet. The joint bouncers just brought

you here about five minutes ago. That's good going even for you, Jake, considering the lick you took with that mug."

He turned with his feet on the floor, letting the dizziness seep out of him. He felt strong again and knew he hadn't been badly hurt. He rubbed his chin reflectively, recalling just about everything, but remembering little Norma Clifton more than anything else.

"What happened to Norma? Where did she go?"

Sabina shrugged indolently. "Oh, she'll be taken care of. Maybe handled a little rough, is all. Turk Munson drove off with her in his new hack, right after the fight. Why is it you're worrying about that little strumpet, anyhow?"

Jake stared at Sabina, a steely glint in his eyes. Anger and resentment stirred in him at her words. An urgent desire to see Norma rose in him. He was certain he didn't want her out in the woods in a hack alone with Brack Mulvane's stepson. He frowned, squeezing his eyes tightly shut. Maybe Sabina Mulvane had a fair question, after all. Why *WAS* he thinking so much about Norma? If any girl should be on his mind, here, this close to home, it should be his betrothed, Trudene Clifton, shouldn't it?

Sabina Mulvane left the room and returned with a pint bottle and a water glass. Instantly, his nostrils caught the pervading, fusel oil blast of moonshine whiskey. But the white liquid made a pleasant gurgling as she poured.

"You want it straight, or with water?"

"Just like it is," he said and drank two jiggers at a gulp. Then suddenly he realized that three years away from the stuff had left him highly vulnerable to moonshine. He coughed violently, opened his mouth to blow out fumes from purgatory and felt hot tears flowing from his eyes. He battled the reaction gamely and finally felt it subside. In its wake came pleasant tentacles of warming, nulling comfort that reached through every nerve. He rose and looked around for his shirt, boots and trousers.

"Jake! What are you fixing to do?"

"I'm pulling out," he said.

"NO! . . . Jake, I told you I wanted to talk with you tonight!"

He forced a smile. "I'm in no humor for talk." He quickly reached for his boots, put on shirt and trousers first, then buckled on his guns.

He rose and faced her. "Thanks for everything. It has been a pretty lively night." He saw his shotgun in a corner. He reached and caught it up.

She rose and rolled herself a smoke.

"Give me a light, will you, Jake?"

He struck one of the big kitchen matches, held it to her cigarette, then broke the match and placed the pieces on a window sill.

"I'll pay for the rooms here as I go out," he said.

"They're already paid for." She gestured to a chair. "Jake, I need to talk business with you. I . . . I want to buy a great portion of the Spaniard family timber rights, and perhaps all your cattle. I want some kind of security when Brack cuts me off."

He shook his head. "I've got big plans for our timber . . . our cattle too."

"I know. My husband must have big plans too. He wants to buy you out. It's one reason a quest has been made to find out when you were coming home . . . But Brack has a finger in almost everything! He doesn't NEED anything else!"

Suspicion knifed through his mind. His cold glance held upon her.

"Hell!" he said with biting scorn. "So Mulvane wants to buy my land and other property, but he figures I hate him too much to do business with him? So he puts you on the lookout for me, and you plan tonight's little enticement to soften me up . . ?"

"Jake! You don't know what you're saying. That's—why, that's silly talk."

"Is it?" A galling fury was in him. "You and your husband Mulvane figured a middle border cracker like me would be easy pickings, didn't you?"

Sabina rose and reached as if to touch him, then withdrew her hand.

"Jake, we can do wonderful things together later if you choose. If I had your native timber and the cattle that roam your ranges, I could do wonderful things for you."

"I'll do things for myself."

But he sensed that she was nervous, almost desperate. It puzzled him. Did she care enough about Brack Mulvane to work this hard for him? Or was Mulvane actually putting the pressure on her?

"Jake, you can't do anything with your wilderness or your cattle without financial help," she said.

"I'll get it."

"I'm afraid you can't. But I KNOW I can."

His full lips flattened. "You shacking up with some banker on the sly?"

He regretted the words instantly. What right did he have to hurl such things in this woman's face? He turned swiftly and looked at a curtained window, then strode across and swept the curtains aside. In the east a full, red moon was rising. Territory trees stood out thickly against the moon. His mind was caught up in a sudden yearning. He had to get out of this room. He needed to be going home to Ma and to Trudene Clifton.

Sabina said softly, "Jake, I see you're determined to leave."

He paused, facing her, and at that moment they heard the whirr and grind of wheels on gravel.

Sabina laughed. "Turk Munson's taken Norma to some moonlight hideout. Now they're headed home."

Jake saw the vague outline of the team and the Spaulding hack in the lantern light turning on the roadway leading toward the Clifton place. His lean jaws clamped. He turned and left. Then, a few minutes later, he was out of the hotel, renting a livery horse at the blind tiger tavern, and riding through the ghostly woodlands toward home. His route was generally in a northeasterly direction, at first following a very old trail toward the junction of Black Fox Creek and Big Skin Bayou. The fork where the creeks joined would no doubt be for years a memorable place for Ma and Lige. Ma had written him about the crowded, colorful and swashbuckling events of the Cherokee Strip payment to Indians that had taken place at the Skin Bayou District Courthouse just a little over a month ago.

"Our one-eighth Cherokee blood got Lige and me three hundred dollars apiece," Ma had written. "It was like the biggest summer picnic I'd ever seen, but it was patrolled by government soldiers. I tried to draw for you, son, but wasn't allowed to. There was hundreds of Indians there, and merchants out of Old Whiskey Smith and Sallisaw got rich quick selling guns, horses, cheap furniture and trinkets to the full bloods. I'd venture that half the full bloods went home broke after Strip Payment Day."

Jake Spaniard tried to visualize the scene as Ma had written it. For a while, he rode with mounting pride in his own one-eighth portion of Indian blood.

It was strange, the way a man could draw strength and assurance by riding on his homeland, no matter whether his early life there had been exceptionally good. Jake's growing up in the Arkansas-Oklahoma border country had been hard, both in the struggle for existence and because of the worries about Pa's whiskey trade. And in later years, after the whiskey war, the troubled, weak-minded condition of his hard-drinking father had been difficult to bear. But time had a way of tempering the bad and heightening the good, he thought as he rode. After three years away, he could ride this dim trail through the region with pleasant memories and a growing exuberance. It was something about the appeal of the Indian land.

The trail followed the erratic course of the dry hummocks above the Big Skin Bayou channel. It wound around in horseshoe bends, rising and dipping, wide enough for a hack or buggy to travel on. In places the road showed a pale yellow in the light of the climbing moon. The night buzzed with swarming insects. The ear-zinging racket of cicadas made a constant, pulsing overtone that swelled against the odd rustling and skittering of fowl and animal life that had spawned in the hills for millions of years. Down in the seeps, he heard bullfrogs tuning up. Jake loved the sounds of the shy night life and the rich smell and feel of the country, after he had left the old hotel. He breathed deeply. The hoofs of the horse crunched steadily, its powerful shoulders and withers making a rhythmic motion as the miles clipped off behind.

He rode with shoulders squared, his face tilted alertly to catch every sound on the wind. He had traveled western Texas and Old Mexico for too long a time with danger always crowding him. It was not sensible to ignore it here, only about a half day's hard ride out of his boyhood hometown of Muldrow, Indian Territory and Whiskey Smith over in Arkansas. Once, suddenly but from a distance, he faintly heard what sounded like the chilling, prolonged womanlike scream of a panther. Again, rounding a bend, he startled a fat wild steer from behind a screen of brush. He thought, "One of these days, it won't be like Ma wrote about her and Lige butchering beef and peddling at the Sequoyah district seat of Sallisaw or over in Whiskey Smith. Wild cattle are still on our land, growing in bigger and bigger herds ever since the day I left. When I get home and rake up funds enough, we'll start drives maybe as far away as Kansas City, and develop our timber production too." Briefly, and though he wouldn't tolerate the thought of doing it, he wondered if there were still any big moonshine whiskey-making in the foothills, as there had been when Pa was active. For a certainty, old Brack Mulvane was getting an almighty lot of whiskey from somewhere. Jake didn't believe it was all bottle in bond from Missouri or Arkansas.

He thought of Ma, no doubt aging some now, maybe burdened with those worries concerning Lige. Poor Lige . . . He was five years older than Jake, and he had sure got himself into some hell that had almost robbed him of his mind during that rustling and whiskey war . . . Jake wondered how Ma and Lige would take it about the murder of old Pa. He'd have to break the news. Jake knew it was going to be hard to tell Ma and

29

Lige that a killer from off the old Choctaw Strip that edged Whiskey Smith had shot Pa in the back. No matter how much trouble Pa had been in and out of, Jake knew Ma had always loved him.

"I don't aim to tell how I was looking for Pa, and the way I found him with his blood running down into the Arkansas River," Jake thought. "I'll try to temper it as much as I can, and not tell how I chased the killer into Fort Smith's Garrison Street and shot him dead when he aimed his shotgun at me."

Spaniard judged by the moon that it was nearing midnight. He began to pass a few ranch shacks and the log or board and batten shanties of poor Cherokee Indians. He wondered if their plight would be any better if Indian Territory was abolished and Oklahoma statehood came. Ah, the flamboyant orators from Washington always tried to fool Cherokees into a belief, but always failed. Ever since the Trail of Tears, the Indians had borne too much.

The trail circled into a grove of oak and cedar and a few scattered pine trees, and just ahead was the Spaniard ranch. On over the ridge to the north was the Clifton home, squalid and lonely on a hump of sandy land. Some semblance of a wagon road began, and Jake saw a house or two that hadn't been there three years before. Beyond the Spaniard house the road circled back toward Sallisaw.

He was heading into the valley of the Spaniard ranch when he heard again the weird, womanlike scream. This time it was close. He halted. He sat in the saddle listening. He wondered if the powerful feline creature had been sneaking through the forest along the road, following him. A faint chill, more of anticipation than of fear, touched his body. Ever since he was a kid, old stories had warned him that the gaunt, black swamp cats, when desperately hungry, would attack a man. He drew his pistol and waited. If the big cat happened to show itself, even momentarily, he knew he could down it with the gun.

When the sound came again, the chill in him mounted. But it was not a chill of anticipation now. He had been gone three years, but close up he could still tell the difference between the sound of a panther's cry and that of a woman screaming. Somewhere on the road just ahead a woman was crying and pleading for help. The startling continuation of the screams seemed to start up the feverish night's rustling and tremors again. Awareness of those things penetrated Jake's senses even as he moved. He dismounted, tied the halter rope of the tavern mount to a sapling, and with a drawn pistol started walking quietly along the road toward the increasingly frantic sounds. He edged to the roadside, where the grass would mute the sound of his footsteps. Then suddenly he saw the halted hack. It was stopped almost squarely in the center of the road, the checklines of the horse team wrapped around the brake. The woman was still screaming. As Spaniard stepped closer, he heard the sound of struggling, and he instantly knew its source. Inside the hack, some man was trying to attack a woman, and she was fighting him.

Tightening his grip on his pistol, Jake eased closer to the hack and in the moonlight, easily recognized it . . . the sleek, phaetonlike vehicle old Brack Mulvane had bought for his stepson three years ago, just before Jake Spaniard had gone to Mexico. Turk Munson had taken Norma Clifton away from the tavern after the brawl as Sabia had said. It must be Norma's screams he was hearing, Jake thought. Norma was inside that hack, battling Turk Munson in a struggle as old as time. A storm of outraged thoughts streaked through Jake Spaniard's mind. But even as the thoughts swirled into his brain, he lunged at the hack and wrenched open the nearest door. . . .

CHAPTER FOUR

"Turk!" he said, with the pent-up hatred of all these years straining through his voice.

The hack grew silent. Jake saw Norma's white face lift beyond Turk's shoulder. Turk Munson cursed.

Jake reached out and grabbed Turk by his burly neck. He hauled him outside the hack and flung him into the road on his back.

"Thank heavens," Jake heard Norma whisper. She came from the hack and stood up facing him, but he wouldn't look at her. He kept his eyes glued to Turk Munson. Mulvane's stepson had many faults and weaknesses, but fear wasn't one of them. Turk was getting up, and Jake knew there was fight in him. There always had been, even back in subscription school ... Turk Munson, liar, cheat, rapist, renegade, but a scrapper. That was Turk.

"Damn you, Spaniard!" Turk raged, swiping a hand at his mouth as he came up and forward.

"What you think you're trying to do to me, man?"

"Get in the hack and beat it!" Jake said. "You do it now, before I blow your brains out or swipe your head off!" Jake thrust out his pistol. "Norma's just a kid!"

It seemed to Jake Spaniard that half his life had been spent either fighting or trying to avoid old Brack Mulvane's no-good stepson. And all the fighting, bloody as it had often been, seemed never to have done any good. Spaniard had never been able to whip Turk Munson, and Turk had never been able to beat him. It had continued as a frustrating and potentially deadly deadstand that probably never would end until one or both of them got killed.

Turk stopped just out of reach, as Jake approached the hack. Quelling the urge to use his pistol as a club, he handed the gun to Norma. "Go home," he told her. "Take the gun with you. I'll pick it up later on."

She took the pistol with a spirited toss of her head and stood looking at Jake. Her eyes shone darkly in the moonlight. "No. I'll hold the gun, but I won't leave you. And you watch Turk. He packs a horrible knife."

Jake glanced at her, comparing her reaction to those he remembered from her sister Trudene under similar moments of strain. Trudene had always seemed hysterically afraid of violence, often stepping between him and some drunken antagonist when trouble broke out, crying and pleading for him not to fight. But Norma wasn't that way. She was of a younger, tougher school. She just took the gun and waited.

"Would you attack a kid, Turk?"

"Kid, hell!" Turk panted. "I'll bust you and have my way yet! You'll see!"

His words brought a drenching wave of relief to Spaniard. He glanced at Norma and saw her fumbling with the torn upper portion of her dress. She had battled and won! Turk Munson hadn't quite made the grade. Spaniard's strength soared at the thought of her fighting spunk.

Turk kept moving toward Jake very slowly, his head doddling a bit like that of an ape, his huge shoulders widening, his fists balling.

"Get out of my way," he growled.

"You beat it, Turk! And stay away from Norma from now on!"

"Bah! Your threats don't scare me none." Turk glanced at Spaniard's pistol. "Where'd you lose your guts? Why don't you get rid of that and stand up to me and fight like a man?"

Jake stood with his lean jaws ridged. He was aware of an almost overwhelming urge to leap at Turk and bash the man's head with a pistol. All the bitter animosity that had built up against Turk Munson over the years seemed to reach its peak. Jake remembered how Turk had cheated at games in school, and the way he had played humiliating tricks behind his back at country dances. Turk had made several passes at Trudene Clifton, too, and had made fun of Jake's

35

brother Lige after Lige had been cruelly beaten over the head during that whiskey war.

Turk said with mounting fury, "I won't need my blade to cut down a goddamn Spaniard! I never did! ... And you'd better be watching which side you're on, you little hussy! ... I'll ..."

Jake's slamming left fist cut Turk's outburst short.

Jake had never had any qualms about getting in the first blow.

Sometimes it meant the difference between a win and a loss in rough-and-tumble backwoods fighting. He followed the left with a right, but Turk was tough and swift. He blocked the blow and smashed a hard-swinging right to Spaniard's head.

Mulvane's mean, unruly stepson had been gifted from childhood with a sledgehammering blow in his right fist. Jake had felt the brunt of that fist many times, but never had its slugging impact been stronger than now. The blow was too high for a knockout, but it rocked Jake sideward against the hack. He welled and straightened, shaking his head to clear it. He saw Turk rushing at him again.

Jake sidestepped and loosed a right into Turk's midsection. It slowed Turk considerably, but didn't stop him. He lunged in savagely, cursing wildly and hurled a swiping left that glanced off Jake's shoulder and grazed the side of his head. Then Turk was in close, and Jake felt the thudding of straight, agonizing blows below his belt. Infighting with this cheating bastard was no good, Jake thought. Turk was like an animal gone berserk, using knees, feet and fists. Jake felt the rise of outrage and a boiling anger that threatened to eliminate clear thought, but he struggled gamely for a cooler head. He backed up, slashed at Turk's face with both fists and felt grimly satisfied as the blows whammed into their mark.

Turk's mad rush slowed. He staggered, then stopped. But only for a moment. Then he was close to Jake again, throwing a vicious left jab that Jake had always had trouble dodging. He ducked this one and countered with a left hook that clipped Turk neatly just under the ear. Turk sucked his breath in like a sledgehammered shoat, his fists dropped, and he sagged weakly against the hack, sliding to his knees. An inborn urge for fair play made Jake wait for Turk to get on his feet again, but Turk didn't rise at once. His breath wheezed loudly in the momentary silence. When he looked up, his eyes had a glassy shine in the moonlight. But he quickly shifted his glance, ferreling like that of a captured wolf.

"Watch him, Jake!" Norma said tensely, and her warning came in the nick of time. Jake realized then that Turk wasn't as badly hurt as he was pretending. He saw Turk's right hand easing into the front pocket of his trousers, questing for his knife.

Jake leaped, and with the toe of his heavy cavalry boot, caught the crook of Turk's arm. The impact jerked Turk's hand from his pocket, and the big bone-handled knife spun across the turf. Turk lurched to his feet, his curses echoing shrilly. He charged Jake again, his rock-hard fists belting into Jake's belly and lower ribs.

It was this kind of brutal attack that had always been hard for Jake to ward off. But now, surprisingly, he found himself absorbing Turk's blows and throwing hard, smashing licks against Turk's face and neck. And suddenly it dawned upon Jake just why he was able to do this. He had been tough, even before that hitch in the Confederate cavalry, but all the rugged training had made him into a man whom Turk Munson's most brutal outlay of strength and trickery could not down.

With a sudden rush of confidence Jake thought, why, I can take this bastard! For the first time in my life, I know I can lay him low! The thought brought a purposeful clarity of mind greater than he had known in years. He began to use every rule and strategy, backing slightly then lunging in, sidestepping and stopping and all the while his left jab thudding against Turk's nose and lips and his right looping in against Turk's face and head. At last he saw his chance and threw an uppercut from knee height that connected soddenly with Turk's forward-tilted chin. Turk's head snapped up and his body fell forward until he hit the gravel face down.

Jake stood over him, breathing hard, waiting. Soft footsteps stirred behind him, and he heard Norma's voice.

"He's had it, Jake. That's enough. Let's go home."

Jake shook his head. "I never could best him. Not until now. I'll wait. I'll make it stick this time."

She moved around until she was between Jake and Turk's sprawled out form. She pushed the cavalry pistol into Jake's holster and took hold of his arms.

"No. Enough is enough. I don't want you to kill a man, Jake."

He said almost harshly, "I've killed plenty men."

"In war, yes . . . yes, I guess you have. But you'd be arrested if you killed Turk now."

"What does Turk Munson mean to you, Norma? You're asking me not to beat his head off. How much does he mean to you?"

Her hands dropped. "Nothing. He doesn't mean a thing to me. I . . . I think I hate him, but he's always hanging around, pestering me. Tonight, after all that trouble, I agreed to let him drive me home. He didn't though; he turned the hack and went toward PawPaw, then wheeled it back past the tavern and finally stopped here on the road . . ."

"I'll haul him up and beat his brains out!"

"No! Jake, he isn't worth getting yourself in trouble with the law!"

Her voice seemed to break through the stupor that gripped Turk's mind. He stirred, his legs scattering gravel. Then he rose to a sitting position and finally weakly gained his feet. She was right, Jake thought, Turk had had it. He staggered around and pulled himself to the seat of the hack. He unwrapped the checklines of the team, his face tilted forward. Then he turned to look at Jake and Norma. His voice came across in a low, threatening growl:

"I'll get even with you two! Time's all I need! I know ways, and I'll make the means. You'll see!"

He slashed at the rumps of the horses with the checklines, turned the hack in a gyrating circle and vanished around a turn.

"He's crazy!" Norma whispered. "He always was, but whiskey is making him worse. He's crazy and dangerous. Oh, Jake, you're going to have to watch out for him now!"

"I guess so." Jake listened to the fading thunder of hoofbeats. "You watch him too. Stay away from him. If I ever hear of him trying to lay a finger on you, I'll shoot him dead."

CHAPTER FIVE

Norma stooped and picked up Turk's bone-handled knife. She straightened, holding the knife and looking steadily at Jake.

"You mean you'd kill Turk, just because he touched me?"

"You know what I mean. I mean if he bothers you, like tonight."

She turned toward the edge of the road, her lithe body poising and her arm going back and forward as she hurled Turk's knife into a sink.

"No other boy ever said a thing like that to me, Jake. All the boys I know, they're on the make, too, and they wouldn't care what Turk Munson does to me."

"Then you'd better make friends with different kinds of boys," Jake said. He glanced back toward his tied horse. "I'll get the mount I rented at the tavern, and you can ride on home."

"I don't need to ride. It's only a little way. You can ride, and I'll walk along beside you."

41

Jake looked at her. "I'll just lead the horse. It's a pretty night for walking, anyhow."

He got the mount and they started walking side by side around the bends. Coils of mist rose from patches of still water. They mingled with the sweat on Jake's clothing. He touched the butt of his pistol and felt its slickness. He unsheathed the gun and tucked it inside his shirt.

Her hand tightened on his arm. She moved closer to him and rose on tiptoe. "Jake."

"Yes?"

"You know how old I am now?"

"Sure. You were about fourteen when I left here. That makes you seventeen now."

Her laughter bubbled out. She did a swift little dance in the road. "Lots of girls get married at seventeen, Jake," she said.

He laughed too, but it was an uncertain, uneasy sound. "I guess you're right. You got a good, steady boyfriend?"

"You're joking. What good, steady boy would want to date a stupid little floozie like me?"

Jake said sharply, "Shut that up! You're pretty and you've been to school some. I can tell by the way you talk."

"Oh, my goodness, yes! I went to subscription school two summers. But I'm still a cheap little country cracker . . . someone for rich women like Sabina Mulvane to laugh at, and for greasy, old beer guzzlers to pinch and paw."

"Just why do you work in a dive like that, Norma?"

"Because I have to help take care of Ma. My

42

pappy stays loaded all the time. He can't work to make a living for us. Old Brack Mulvane's greedy ways took all the sap out of Pa."

"Your Pa didn't drink so much three years ago."

She laughed mockingly. "When a man thinks he's licked for good it grows on him, that urge for drinking. Haven't you ever noticed that?"

The bitterness in her voice intensified his uneasiness. They started on. Houses and cleared patches of land came into view. He said abruptly, "You know, I think I'll go right to the house with you, Norma. I'd like to see Trudene right now."

"You mean get her out of bed this late?"

"Why not?"

She said shortly, "I don't think Trudene would appreciate you waking her. Really. She's . . . well, Trudene has changed some, Jake."

"How?"

"She's moody, serious-minded, burdened about something, it seems."

"She was always a little that way, Norma."

"Maybe. But it's worse now. Jake, Pa was drunk when I left for work. I wish you wouldn't go in."

"All right. I just had the urge, that's all. Will you tell Trudene to meet me tomorrow, about midmorning? Down by the old sawmill stand where we used to meet. Will you tell her that?"

"Yes."

They were at the turnoff to the Clifton home. They stopped. Norma kept holding Jake's arm.

He said with all the cheerfulness he could muster. "Take care of yourself, young'un. And tell Trudene I'm wanting to see her, real bad."

She quickly released his arm, and he watched her turn away and finally vanish beyond a cluster of small elm trees. The moon was still bright. He could have seen her if she had looked back at him and waved, but she didn't. She hurried on. He mounted and rode, but somehow he felt he was in a bad way, like a man lost and alone in a strange world without clear horizons. He was still that way several minutes later when he came in sight of home.

He stopped on a rise of land and looked down in the moonlight on the old clapboard house. He was surprised that without adequate funds all these years the old house wasn't badly weathered or in dire need of fast repairs. The clapboards glistened with what appeared to be a brand new coat of paint, and the split oak shakes atop the roof were new. Two more cupolas had been added, and down on a drop-off on the western end of the house, another room of board and batten had been added, evidently of yellow pine. A new paled fence surrounded the yard. Lige was probably holding his own pretty well if he had split those pales and built that fence, Jake thought.

He had stopped the tavern horse and continued to let his eyes wander. He noticed the well-trimmed shrubbery and the blooming flowers in the front yard. Old memories swarmed around him. Ma had always loved pretty flowers.

Only the horse and cattle corrals and the big log barn and hay sheds appeared the same, but they were in good repair. Near the enclosure for the steers, a small new building had been constructed. That small building would be for cutting up butchered beef, Jake guessed. He pictured in his mind his brother Lige's big hands, handling sliced-off portions of a freshly killed steer.

Then Jake's glance centered upon the barn's long and shadowy hallway. Even in the dimming light of the lowering moon, a vehicle with a new look seemed to appear. He nudged the horse with boot heels and rode on down. The vehicle in the hallway of the barn was a new Springfield wagon, it's shiny tongue hoisted aloft and propped up for protection against any dampness or mud. Suddenly Jake Spaniard noticed something else too—a big span of mules on a ranch where mules had never been seen before. The mules looked young, strong, sleek, standing with ears pointed alertly as he rode up.

Why, there was prosperity here on the old home place, Jake thought. And the disturbance Norma Clifton had roused in him gradually faded. He was aware again of growing exuberance. After three years away on the arid plains of far west Texas and amid the comparative poverty in many places of Mexico, he could feel nothing except vast pride at what Lige and Ma had held together and improved. But then he felt a jolt of sadness as he remembered the course of his own life. Circumstances and a hot temper had made him a gunman, while Ma and Lige had stayed peacefully on the old home ranch despite Pa's renegade ways. They had worked hard and determinedly to improve the place, and they'd done very well for themselves. That was plain to see.

He pulled up at the barnyard gate, dismounted and led the horse insid and unsaddled and fed it. Lige's old mongrel foxhound, long and gaunt as always because nothing would fatten him, trotted around a corner of the barn on heavy pads and stopped. The hound lowered his head in an odd way, twisting it sideward and watching Jake.

"Padge!" Jake said softly, snapping his fingers. "Padge, ol' boy!"

Old Padge went flat on his belly, his hind legs straight out, his tail switching up a little storm of dust and leaves as he recognized Jake's voice. The hound didn't approach Jake though. Padge was a one-man dog . . . Lige Spaniard's dog. Then, as Jake went on toward the house, the old hound drew himself up slowly, planted his forepaws far out in front of his crouching hindquarters, lifted his heavy-jowled muzzle straight up and began to bawl sadly at the moon.

Jake was at the stoop of the porch when he heard the front door of the house squeak open and saw Lige step out onto the porch. Lige was pulling on a pair of overalls and snapping the galluses across his naked shoulders. For a moment, he peered at Jake, then he ran a hand through his disheveled black hair and turned his head. "Ma," he said. "Ma, Jake's home."

Jake went forward, laughing happily and offering his hand.

"Sure good to see you, Lige ... good to be home again."

"I guess so," Lige said. At first his callused, work-toughened hand had a strong, warm clasp, but suddenly it went limp and dropped away. He went around Jake and swung off the porch into the yard.

The gaunt hound was still mournfully baying the moon, the sound rolling off in belling echoes through the woods.

"Stop that!" Lige said commandingly. When the hound obeyed and slunk around the house, Jake saw Lige following, the legs of his overalls flapping about his bare ankles. Lige was headed for the barn or for the little outhouse, Jake thought. He started on toward the doorway and saw Ma appear.

"Jake, son!" she breathed, hurrying out with upflung hands. He grabbed her, feeling her thin arms in a bulky nightgown hugging him with surprising strength.

He felt the moisture of tears when she pressed her face against his cheek. But later, after she had led him into the house and fired up a coal oil lamp, her eyes looked dry and happy. Ma had good control that way, he knew. She wouldn't even cry much when he told her about Pa's death, Jake guessed ... Ma had strength, physically and spiritually. She had the fortitude to bear silently the things she couldn't help. It was

47

good to look at her and to know she was holding up well. Evidently, worry hadn't borne her down much during the past three years.

"Ma, you look younger than you did three years ago," Jake said as he took a chair.

"I ain't wantin' any of your flattery, Jake Spaniard," she returned, laughing. She stood with her hands on her hips, her sharp eyes measuring him. "You've had yourself a fight tonight, ain't you, boy?"

"Yep. Two," Jake said.

Her glance held an instant on his swollen chin where the beer mug had struck. "Well, you didn't get bloodied up much." She walked halfway around him. "You know, you're almost as big as your pa was. I don't guess you'd have to take much off any man. Your pa never did."

"You said once that Pa liked to fight. I don't."

"Phooey," she scoffed. "You want something to eat?"

"Not now. Just a good soft bed . . . Ma, how's Lige making out?"

"He's fine. He's been happy and normal as any man, all this year," Ma said, but Jake didn't like the way she abruptly turned from him. "I'll fluff up your pillows a bit, son. Then you can get to bed."

Jake sat in the dim lamplight as she left the room. He looked around at all the familiar furnishings—things he had known ever since he was a child: straight-backed oak chairs, splint-bottomed, a huge leather sofa that Pa had bought Ma after an unusually lucrative whiskey deal, a big dresser with a square mirror that had come into the family secondhand but was still durable enough to last another hundred years. There were some pictures of Ma and Pa's parents on the wall, and an old *Farmer's Almanac,* and one small painting of a waterfall. A big oval-topped clock that had been in the family as long as the dresser stood on a shelf high against the northern wall. Jake thought with mounting happiness, we'll store these old heirlooms and get new furnishings when the money starts coming in from my cattle drive and all the pine timber I aim to sell. . . .

Lige returned almost soundlessly and took a chair near Jake. He was a big, heavy-bodied man, but broader and possibly stronger in an awkward way. At least he had been strong as an ox before that whiskey war. But his face, though browned from almost constant exposure to the Oklahoma sun, looked a bit too sensitive for that of a backwoods man. The truth was . . . and it had always been that way . . . Lige Spaniard didn't have the aggressive constitution that his bigness implied. His eyes, gray like Ma's but not as shrewd and piercing, had a dreamy, faraway look that had always puzzled Jake.

"Lige, how are the cattle herds?" Jake asked. "I noticed the new wagon and everything. It looks like you and Ma are doing real good here."

"I don't mess around with any of them damn wild bulls. I grow things to eat and sell . . . vegetables and things in my clearing. Butcher and sell beef too."

"Where's any market for produce?"

"In Sallisaw. The town's building up. Lots of eastern speculators comin' in."

"Speculators for what?"

"I ain't certain. Maybe for coal, or this new black oil that is almost right on the top of the ground. Or maybe they're whiskey buyers . . . Don't know."

"Doesn't seem right, Lige . . . the Spaniards not working cattle."

"You can have that . . . if you stay here. You aim to stay?"

The question had a strange, waiting intensity in it that Jake didn't understand.

"I expect to stay, Lige. Sure I do."

Lige got up and wandered around the room, looking down at the floor as if searching for the answer to some puzzling question, as if the answer was there right at hand but still unreachable.

"Well, I wondered if you'd stay," he said. "Lots of the fellows, back from the Strip Run . . . they don't stay here in the country. They go to the big towns to find good jobs."

"I'm not that way, Lige. I like the country . . . all the outdoors. And I've got some mighty big plans for our cattle herds and our groves of pines. I'm going to raise funds from Sallisaw banks to get some projects on the road. Why, we might almost get to be rich folks, you never can tell!"

Jake paused, aware that Ma had returned and was standing in the bedroom doorway, listening.

She didn't say anything. Neither did Lige. He turned and left for the side room where he always slept.

"Bed's ready, Jake," Ma said. "You stretch out and rest good now."

Jake smiled, rose and went past her, touching her thin shoulder affectionately. But long before he went to sleep that night, his thoughts hovered around the dread that Lige's mind wasn't so good, after all.

CHAPTER SIX

That dread was still on Jake Spaniard's mind next morning while he worked with Lige and Ma, butchering a prime beef for market. Ma had told Jake the night before that she and Lige intended to butcher in the morning and that Lige would haul the beef to stores in Sallisaw.

"I'll pitch in and help for a while, before I take that rented horse back," Jake had said. "Ma, is Sallisaw growing much?"

"Yes. Mighty fast. No longer an Indian settlement. More whites swarming in all the time, crowding out the Cherokees. Most of the full bloods, them known as 'Old Settlement People' have gone back to the woods around Belfonte, Dwight Mission, old Walking Stick Hollow or Stilwell. Brack Mulvane is the major leader that's helping to crowd the Indians out."

"That would figure," Jake said.

He watched his brother occasionally as Lige worked with the beef. Lige appeared efficient, his strong hands deft and certain as he packed the meat so attractively in hope of faster sale. But Lige's reluctance to talk to him worried Jake Spaniard. It seemed that every time Jake spoke, Lige became highly nervous and got even more busy, as if determined to workup a sweat and shake it off. Now and then, just for an instant, Lige paused and glanced along the road toward the Clifton place, as if expecting someone to arrive.

The butchering was finished and all salable meat packed and loaded into the wagon before midmorning. "Lige, I'd like to go help you sell this," Jake said. "But I have to take the horse back, and I'm supposed to meet Trudene pretty soon."

Lige sat on the seat of the wagon, wiping sweat from his face. Jake noticed that his brother's hands were shaking. Lige had worked too hard in the heat, Jake thought. Suddenly there was an urge in Jake to let even the meeting with Trudene wait . . . to send Ma to tell her, so he could side Lige on this trip to town . . . side his brother through anything.

"Thanks," Lige said. "But all this stuff is contracted for. It won't be much of a job." He didn't look at Jake. Watching his eyes in profile, Jake could see they were throwing Lige's gaze into the far distance, quivering like the heat-haze that danced across the woods and fields. Then Lige looked at Ma, who was kneeling in the shade of an oak tree, sorting again through culled beef cuts, picking out the best ones for canning or home use. "You might ask Ma if she'd like a trip to town," Lige said.

Jake nodded and hurried over to Ma. "Lige wants you to go with him, Ma. He seems . . . disturbed about something."

Ma rose calmly. She didn't say anything. She brushed off her dress, glanced down at her dusty shoes, touched her gray hair where it was rolled against the nape of her neck, then walked to the wagon and stepped up to the seat beside Lige. She waved at Jake with a cheerful gesture, but as he watched the wagon vanish toward Sallisaw, he was overcome by a strange, oppressive feeling. He knew no happiness as he walked to the house to wash up for the meeting with Trudene.

Thinking of possible hostility in the region, he rode down cautiously to the old sawmill stand. The heaps of sawdust had blackened more and flattened out some during his absence. Dirt, rain-swept leaves and brush had half filled the pit where the circular saw had once shrilled its vicious swath through green pine logs on the carriage. Yonder, where huge slabs of off-fall had shone white and yellow in the sun three years ago, there was now nothing but a pile of rot. Beetles and ants stirred there, and worms writhed in it. Creepers, vines, and patches of poison ivy were moving in. The clean sawdust had vanished completely, consumed and blighted by dampness and passing time. It wasn't a good place to meet a girl, Jake thought. There wasn't any place to sit, not even a clean white scantling.

He was late, and he half expected to see

Trudene there ahead of him, but evidently she hadn't arrived. He dismounted, tied the horse and walked over the spongy, rotting sawdust heap. His boots sank deep into soggy deadness. He walked around for a while, restlessly, hitting his balled fists lightly together, liking the slight feeling of pain. Stones of the furnace, where roaring fires had once blazed under a trembling, monstrous boiler, were now almost hidden by weeds and brush. It was lonely here, and Jake felt lonely and despondent. He reckoned it was all tied up in the sight of change that he hadn't noticed in his younger years. It wasn't pleasant to suddenly become aware of irrevocable change and the swiftness of passing time . . . things a man couldn't do anything about, regardless of his strength of will. Jake thought with sudden insight, I guess it's taken me twenty-two years to grow up . . .

A silent, turgid heat filled the woodlands at this time of day, when the high sun had scorched all the mists away and the belts of pines stood like sentinels in the garish light. He knew it was better far back in the virgin forests of Spaniard land where moisture stayed captured and gold, green and bronze grass grew lush for roving herds of cattle. There a man could pick out fickle courses on hummocks of grazing land and know the spine-tingling seizure of adventure, the feeling of being part and parcel of a place where time had little meaning for an ambitious, hard-riding cattleman.

Suddenly Jake turned about, aware of a

presence. He grinned. From behind one of the pines, stepped Trudene Clifton, walking slowly, her hands locked tightly across the front of her blue print dress. There had always been an ethereal beauty about her, no matter where Jake had seen her, day or night. He went to meet her, conscious more than ever of that breath taking beauty that had always drawn so much tenderness out of him. She was a tall girl, almost willowy, but there was a certain strength and virility about the way she moved. Her hair was black and long, reaching down past her shoulders. Her eyes, darker than her sister Norma's, held a reaching brilliance as she stood looking at him.

Jake was a bit disturbed at the way she stood there, unsmiling, almost expressionless. In the old days, when they had met here, there had been an eagerness, a rush, a wide throwing of arms to hold each other. Now, when he moved closer to her, he noticed that her face was pale and wan, and he sensed a reluctance in her. Norma had been right, he thought. Trudene had changed, and it was a more definite change than Jake had expected.

"Trudene!" he said, and started to take her in his arms. But she backed up and reached out to grab both his hands, avoiding his embrace.

"Jake, you'll have to forgive me, I guess."

"For what?"

"I got here early. I've been a-hidin', back there in them trees. I've been watchin' you. I guess I oughtn't to of did that, ought I?"

"Why, it's all right." He forced a smile, thinking of her backwoods talk. He remembered that Trudene had never attended school and was surprised he didn't like it. All through his riding, back there in Mexico, he had remembered her talk and longed for the sound of it, but now it irritated him. She couldn't talk English as well as an educated Mexican girl. But absorbing a little education, and taking up more conventional talk didn't change people, did it? Hell, he was noted as a high-tempered young gunfighter whose hangout had been Old Whiskey Smith, wasn't he?

He swept Trudene's hands aside and took her in his arms. He kissed her, but her lack of response made him frustrated, disappointed. What had happened to her? What had come between them? Her sister Norma had stirred more passion in him on that old forest road last night.

Abruptly Jake straightened and released her. He thought he knew what was wrong. Norma had told Trudene about Sabina Mulvane. Knowledge of Jake's infidelity was crushing Trudene's spirit. His splurge with Sabina Mulvane was having its repercussions . . . hurting the girl he loved. Damnit, why had he let himself get involved? Why had he caused this hurt?

"Jake, I ain't got but a minute to stay," Trudene said. She stepped back from him. "Mom's sick, and Pa ain't feelin' well. Norma wrote me a note before she went to bed last night, though, sayin' you was back and wanted to see me. I felt like I ought to come."

Jake looked at her, frowning, and finally took the plunge. "What else did Norma write you in that note?"

Trudene's eyes widened slightly. "Nothing. She just scribbled that you were back and wanted to see me here at the mill."

"You didn't talk to Norma this morning?"

"No. She works nights, you know. She sleeps pretty late in the day. I didn't think I ought to rouse her . . . I don't guess I'd of felt right if I hadn't come here, you bein' gone so long an' all."

Jake smiled. "I'd think not. The girl I aim to marry wouldn't be expected to dodge me, would she, now?"

Trudene's dark glance moved about the woodland, then steadied to meet his gaze. "Jake, I've got to think about this marryin'," she said.

"You mean about us? About our plans?"

She nodded. "Jake, you've been gone a long time."

"What does it matter? What about the things we promised each other? What about all those good things we talked about . . . And why didn't you write me?"

"Oh, I wouldn't of hurt you by letters, Jake, and you off there so far."

He said in a level voice, "I came back with intentions for us to get married soon, but if you've met someone else . . . ?"

He stopped at the desperate look on her face. "I told you I've got to think, Jake. That's all I said. I'll get back to the house now, and I'll think. And you be thinking too. You hear?"

"When will I see you again?" he asked.

"I don't know. I just don't rightly know."

"Two days? Three?" he pressed.

"Give me three days, Jake. Then I'll meet you here, same time."

"All right."

He stood with narrowed eyes and watched Trudene hurry off through the pine grove. Trudene was right, he thought. He needed to do some thinking too. He hoped they could iron out the queerness in their relationship in three days' time.

He centered his attention then on a sandhill crane that stood preening itself between two twisted pines. He stooped and grabbed up a handful of damp sawdust and hurled it at the bird. "Shoo-oo!" he yelled.

He reached the tavern horse and mounted, burdened with conflicting thoughts. He was almost certain that Norma had told Trudene about Sabina Mulvane. It was hurting Trudene's pride, he thought, and she would evade him until she was satisfied that he had suffered enough for his mistake.

He sat the horse a moment without traveling, liking the feel of the saddle, liking the way the horse held its head high with pointed ears. He hadn't thought about it before, but now he considered the silver in his pocket and figured he might buy this mount. The horse was proving good.

He sat on the saddle quietly, knowing his

thoughts were getting scattered. That was strange. He saw a hawk sailing high in the elements, riding the currents of the wind. He knew he had to collect his thoughts and be honest with himself. He had to face up to things like a man. That thing about Sabina Mulvane . . . he realized he wasn't nearly as concerned about that as he was about the way thoughts of Norma Clifton kept intruding on his old dream of Trudene. What was he going to do about that? He reached up, jerked off a pine frond and slapped it against his leg. He was restless, frustrated. He needed something solid to pin his thoughts down strong. He surely still loved Trudene, even though she had been evasive and distant with him. He had an obligation to her. He couldn't slough off that obligation and come out whole again like a damned snake shedding its skin.

"People have more trouble than anybody," he muttered, then grinned at the old quip and turned his mount up the trail.

But when he came within sight of the junction with the Sallisaw road, he saw a team and a dust-covered vehicle moving swiftly toward the Spaniard homestead. He wondered, at first, if Ma and Lige were returning from town. But he knew they couldn't be. They would be in Sallisaw for hours. Then he saw that the vehicle was a huge phaeton, black with glittering metal trimming. It was slowing and stopping in front of the Spaniard House. Jake sent the horse that way. Two men were in the phaeton: a hulking, stoical-faced driver and a gray-haired man who was putting on a wide straw hat as he opened the door on his side. Jake Spaniard was within a few feet of the phaeton, and he recognized the man even before the man stepped out and pulled himself haughtily erect. It was Brack Mulvane.

CHAPTER SEVEN

The long years of Mulvane's life had sat lightly upon him. The fact was in itself enough to grind a deeper and more consuming resentment and hatred into Jake Spaniard. Mulvane was the suave, unruffled conniver who manipulated people, forced them into situations which made them protect him and bear the brunt when he made mistakes. He had never known what it was to do a lick of work, like toting hundred-pound sacks of sugar and bran through waist-deep water, breaking way to hidden whiskey stills that his "cracker" hirelings had operated for him. And Mulvane had never known what it was to sweat out months in the federal prisons after laws had been passed against selling whiskey to Arkansas-Oklahoma Indians. He always sweet-talked his hirelings into taking the rap, maybe threatening their families with violence from his thugs if they didn't cooperate. Then there was the time, just before the whiskey war, when Mulvane had given himself up to a crooked judge whose palm he had warmed. He had managed to squirm free after laying the blame for whiskey-running on Jake Spaniard's Pa. All those thoughts spawned bitter memories in Jake as he stopped the horse and watched Brack Mulvane step forward.

"Jake, it's a pleasure!" Mulvane said, smiling blandly and offering up his hand.

Jake glanced coldly at Mulvane's hand and didn't offer to take it. He felt an urge to slap the hand aside. Instead, he dismounted and deliberately shifted the weight of the gun at his hip.

"What is it you want here, Mulvane?" he demanded.

Mulvane's hand went up to a pocket of his white shirt. He took out an expensive cigar, but stood rolling it lightly between thumb and forefinger without lighting it. Finally he fired it up, but still stood silently, watching Jake. Mulvane had a way about him that seemed to cling to some men of power. It was a nonchalant aloofness that he asserted when a friendly approach didn't take too well. He always contained his temper, never displaying brash anger like Pa had always done, often lashing out at the judge and lawmen in court.

Mulvane, though well past sixty, was a smooth-featured and handsome man, broad and square-built, straight-nosed and full-lipped, black-eyed and strong. It had been said that he had been a devil to the women in his young and middle years. Or maybe he still was, Jake thought, if he was wanting a woman more beautiful and younger than Sabina. Mulvane looked at the old Spaniard home, and around at the barn and sheds, and on out to the vegetable fields beyond.

"Your Ma and Lige have a good setup here," he finally said, but when he spoke, he deliberately looked at the squalid, little outhouse, and his contempt for the family showed in the curling of his lips.

Evidently the man driving the phaeton had been watching his boss. Now he suddenly snickered and held his nose. Fury swarmed in Jake Spaniard. He hadn't the sligthest desire to conceal it. He wrapped the reins of the horse around a sapling and his long stride took him away from Brack Mulvane and straight toward the hulking man in the phaeton. Jake pointed to the outhouse.

"We've got a big trench behind it, slob!" he said. He wrenched open the door of the phaeton. "Get out! We'll walk over, you and me and I'll just toss you in like the stinking carrion you are!"

"Spaniard," Brack Mulvane said. His voice hadn't lifted a whit, but there was warning in it. Jake stiffened as the man in the phaeton twisted sideward. The man looked up at Jake out of cold, heavy eyes. In his hand was a cap-and-ball pistol, its bore gaping straight into Jake's face. Jake knew the man had the pistol there in his lap the whole time.

"Why don't you be a little more sociable,

Spaniard?" Brack Mulvane said. "You're touchier than your Pa used to be ... Pull the door shut now, Rupe."

Jake battled his galling fury, knowing he had to keep a clear head or get himself shot down.

"State your business, Mulvane," he said. "Then get out!"

Mulvane smiled. "Why I just dropped by to see you folks about that big belt of pine timber down near the creek. I'd like to buy that land."

"That's one stretch of pine trees that no man's going to buy," Jake snapped. "Not until I get ready! And I sure won't sell it to you!"

"Aw, come again, boy. Anything has a price."

Jake knew he was rubbing the man the wrong way now. He liked it. He forced a grin.

"I'll cut and sell that timber and develop the slopes into grazing land," he said. "I kind of like the challenge of doing that, after so much shooting and fighting during that whiskey-rustler war you caused among your men and my Pa."

"It's going to be a mighty expensive operation, though." Mulvane's voice was very quiet.

"I've done some figuring on that, Mulvane, and I know I can raise the money. The Spaniard family never wanted for friends ... not even some big-rich families in town."

Mulvane smoked his cigar, rolling it from side to side between his lips. "Sure. Sure," he said. "Men like Elmer Gordon, now. He was a good friend of the Spaniard family, I heard."

"What do you mean ... WAS?" Jake demanded.

Mulvane shrugged. "Well, Elmer isn't living now," he said.

The driver of the phaeton suddenly laughed, and it struck Jake's ears with a dribbling finality, like the sound of pebbles dropping into a still, dark pool.

"Turn the vehicle around, Rupe," Mulvane ordered. He blew cigar smoke toward Jake, just like no one was there. "Well, if you won't sell, you just won't sell, I reckon. But since my lease on the timber has expired . . . or is going to be expiring pretty soon, just thought I'd drop around and see . . . "

Jake interrupted harshly, "Lease?"

"Oh, yes. Hasn't your mother told you. I leased the timber and even the swampland from your Ma and Lige, not long after you left here three years ago."

"That's a lie!"

The driver had pulled the phaeton up beside the barnyard gate and was backing and turning it. Mulvane glanced that way fleetingly, and when he faced Jake again, he saw the big cavalry pistol almost against his belly.

"You're a liar and cheat!" Jake gritted. "And your driver can't shoot true enough with that old cap and ball to take me before I take you! . . . Go get the hell inside that thing and move on out of here!"

Brack Mulvane's lips looked thin and without the color of blood, but he moved, gestured for the driver to open the door of the phaeton for him. At Mulvane's tight order, the driver cracked a whip, and the team and phaeton moved away in the direction they had come. Jake decided to let the horse stand for a while tied to the sapling. He went to the house and sat down on the stoop of the porch. From somewhere beyond the clearing he heard the hoarse, victorious yelp of Lige's hound. That sound was quickly followed by the thin, chilling death cry of a rabbit. The sounds rushed through Jake and knocked some of the seething anger out of him. He pictured the hound's long jaws with snaggy teeth clamping down on the body of the rabbit, bursting its entrails, cracking its spine. A faint unease stirred in him. He got up and paced restlessly across the yard. In the distance he could still hear the hoofbeats of the team hitched to Brack Mulvane's phaeton. Evidently, the vehicle had turned right after disappearing over the first hummock, going past the Clifton place instead of back into Pawnee on the south portion of the looping road.

The heat of midday approached, and Jake finally went again to the shade of the porch. He was impatient for Ma and Lige to return, so he could find out if Mulvane had been telling the truth about that lease. But it might be hours before they came back. Abruptly, he rose and headed into the edge of the forest. He needed to get out where the pine trees stood high against the cobalt sky. He needed to start figuring the best way to get that fine timber out to market, and the most sure-fire method of gathering wild herds of cattle and heading them north. Jake was walking beneath the hot, bright sun in a small, open meadow when he heard a familiar voice call to him. He turned, aware of a breathless feeling, and saw Norma Clifton hurrying toward him along a nearby forest aisle.

CHAPTER EIGHT

She was as pretty in the revealing daylight as she was in the dim tavern that night, Jake Spaniard thought. He stood with mounting happiness, watching her approach. Why, the little trick knew how to dress as well as the elite for the outdoors, he thought. She could pass for the daughter of some rich eastern family spending a fishing vacation along Big Skin Bayou or the clear blue water of Sallisaw Creek. She was wearing a loose-fitting brown and white polka dot dress and her small feet were encased in soft, Indian beadwork sandals.

"Norma, you're pretty as a speckled pup," he said as she stopped, confronting him.

She smiled with a flash of white teeth. "You talk silly, Jake. But I like it. . ."

He took her outstretched hand, but only briefly. The disturbance he felt by her presence made him flush.

"Jake," she said chidingly. "I believe you're

afraid of me."

He forced a laugh. "I don't think so, but you could be right. One thing I do know is you're like tea or tonic Ma used to make from Mayapple roots."

"Oh, I HATE that stuff!" she declared.

"Maybe the taste. But it's the good way it makes you feel that counts."

She turned away abruptly and sat down on a mossy bank.

"Sit down, Jake," she said. "To tell you frankly, I'm worried about U. S. marshals or the Cherokee Lighthorse coming in here. Rumors are out that you killed a man in Old Whiskey Smith."

His lips tightened as he sat down beside her, stretching out his long legs with their scuffed and scarred old high-heeled boots.

"Jake, you're becoming known as a very dangerous gunman," she pressed. "I can't bring myself to think that's good."

"I don't want anybody to think it's good," he said. "I don't think it's good either. I have bad dreams about men I've shot, but I have to get hold of myself, because I know that every time I've pulled my pistol, it was in self-defense."

"Jake, why is it that sometimes you wear two guns and other times only one?"

He was hesitant to tell her, wondering if she would understand. Then he said quietly, "It's an idea I came up with that I thought might give me a split-second advantage over the fastest enemy . . . Let him see me with two guns on, then surprise him with only one in sight. Or the other way around, you see . . . one gun, and then at showdown time, I appear with two . . . A small change, but I don't think it's one to be ignored."

"Jake, you aren't a professional killer! . . . Why, I couldn't possibly love a man that went out and killed for money!"

"Aw, don't say things like that, Norma! Of course I'm far from a professional gun-fighter! . . . And that thing about love . . . I'm at least eight years older than you, and there's Trudene . . ."

She went rigidly still for an instant, then said in a tremulous voice, "You're going to have to forget about Trudene, Jake. I don't feel that you love her. And I KNOW she doesn't love you!"

Jake stood up, confronting her. "How can you say things like that?"

"Because I KNOW!" she insisted. "You may think this brazen, but if you really love either of us Clifton girls, it's me!"

He turned his gaze away from her, but was aware that she had stood up too. For several seconds, he stared off through the forest. From a nearby meadow, he heard the resounding bawl of a range land bull. The sound seemed to tap against the tree trunks, echoing away for miles.

"You go home, Norma. It isn't right, us being alone here this way."

She moved and caught his left hand. "It's right if we make it right and keep it so."

"You don't know what you're saying! It's like I told you. You're just a kid."

She released his hand and stepped back, and

he turned slightly to look at her. "Turk Munson doesn't think I'm a kid," she said. "And do you think a girl can get a job in one of Brack Mulvane's places if she's just a child?"

"I don't want to hear such things! Shut up!"

"Well, I know you don't, and I know the reason, Jake. It's the way I felt last night when I saw you with Sabina Mulvane, or when I know you're going to be with Trudene. You see, I love you too. And you don't love Trudene anymore, do you, Jake?"

"You shouldn't be talking things like that!"

"Why not? . . . Jake, even before you went off to Mexico . . . all those times you came to our house to court Trudene, didn't you ever wonder why I always ran off into the woods or out in the dark? I couldn't bear to see you with Trudene! I almost hated her, my own sister . . ."

"Norma, you were just a little tyke of a girl."

She lifted her face determinedly. "Size or age doesn't make any difference! Not if someone really loves a person and it grows all through the years. My own mother has told me that, lots of times."

"If she did it wasn't good raising."

Her gaze riveted on his face. "You don't believe love for a person can grow, Jake? Is that what you mean?"

"I mean a girl shouldn't be tampering with men, the way you're tampering with me! More country girls in the backwoods have got themselves in trouble in cases like this than I could ever name!"

Her hand flashed up, touching his lips. "You've come home, Jake, and I can mean more to you than my sister ever will. She doesn't love you the way I do, Jake! Please believe me! You're going to have to stop thinking about my sister Trudene!"

Suddenly she moved against him, her arms reaching around Jake's neck. Her lips first touched his cheek, then pulled around to meet his own lips. No man could resist such urgency. He wrapped her up and held her close. But long and careful thoughts could strike a man's mind, Jake Spaniard found, even while holding a young girl in his arms. Finally he released her and held her away at arm's length, intently searching her eyes. She wasn't crying openly, but the sting of tears was there, pressing against her eyelids. She said huskily, "Jake, your mother will tell you why you must forget Trudene ... that Trudene has long since given her heart to someone else."

"Why hasn't Ma told me before now?"

"I don't know. Maybe she dreads hurting you ... But whatever she tells you, I don't want you to make a decision about me on that alone. I don't want to be second best. If you don't love me ... don't think you could ever learn to love me, tell me now."

Jake held her hands and pulled her down to a resting place beside him on the mossy bank. For several minutes he stayed quiet, silently thinking about Trudene's actions at the old mill stand and remembering that though she had been in possession of his address, she had not written him during the years he had been gone. . . . Jake Spaniard was a man without hesitation, once he figured his course was clear. He knew he had to believe Norma Clifton. He suddenly also recognized the disturbance that had prevailed in him since first sight of Norma in the tavern.

He faced her squarely at last. "I wouldn't have to LEARN to love you, Norma," he said. "I know I DO love you, and I'll face it and ask you to be my wife."

He spoke of his love for her. He would be good to her. He would do things for her, all the rest of his days. But he was disturbed by the uneasy look in her eyes.

"Jake, I wish you'd reconsider . . . Forget about your plans here, at least for a while, and go away."

"You scoot off home and stop worrying about Mulvane's threats."

He saw her force a smile. "You come to see me often, Jake . . . you big lug! And you be careful, hear me? You're a scrapper, but a bullet or a knife blade in the back are hard to fight."

He returned her smile and watched her circle toward home, and it occurred to him that she had asked him to go away because of Trudene. That was it, he thought. Norma wouldn't be worried about what Brack Mulvane would do. She was worried about what her sister Trudene would think. Jake knew he was worried too. It was a growing thing in his mind as he reached the tavern horse, mounted and took the road through the woodlands. It was a nagging self-condemnation that wouldn't let him rest. A man soared to the peak of bliss, often unthinking or with deliberate abandon, but he always paid the price. No matter how much he thought of Norma, he had first obligated himself to Trudene. His love for Norma had to be the one thing that would make things right.

He decided to purchase the tavern horse as he traveled, providing the price wasn't too high. He knew the many ponies of the Spaniard family had long since gone wild in the region, just like the cattle in Pa's big herd. He found that the price of the bay horse was reasonable, but he kept a keen eye on loungers and passersby as the transaction in cash was made. He knew there were bunches of riffraff in this part of Oklahoma who would slit a man's throat for a dime. The tavern area and the hotel looked squalid in the daylight. He was relieved to be mounted and on the return junket home.

Ma and Lige had returned from Pawnee. Jake saw them beside the halted wagon near the barn. As he approached, Lige lifted his head, and there was an odd shine in his eyes that made Jake wonder if he had startled his brother. Then Jake stopped the bay. He noticed a strange look in Ma's eyes too, a deep sadness or something. It was the same kind of worry he had seen earlier in the day in Norma Clifton's concerned glance. He wondered if Brack Mulvane had confronted Ma and Lige in town and made any threats.

"Market good today, Ma?" he finally asked.

"Yes . . . yes, it was fine."

Jake looked at Lige again, who had un-harnessed the team under the hallway of the barn. Lige finished the chore, dumped corn to the team, then slammed the crib door shut and struck out across the fields toward the woods. Jake could see him plainly, a big stooped shape striding swiftly. Lige disappeared.

Jake dismounted. "Ma, Lige isn't much better, is he now?"

For a while she didn't answer. She looked at Jake, then at the dark wall of forest into which Lige had disappeared.

Finally she murmured, "No, I don't guess Lige is much better. He was, but he ain't right now."

"What's disturbed him, Ma?" Jake led the bay toward the barnyard gate. "Has my coming back made him think again about that old whiskey war or about the big war that took Pa's life?"

"No, I don't think it has anything to do about warring or anything like that. Lige got over that . . . Son, have you been out in the woods with Trudene Clifton, all this time?"

Jake scraped a boot toe in the dirt. "No," he said at last. "I wasn't with Trudene very long. I rode to the old tavern stand and bought this horse."

"We just saw you, coming along the road . . ."

"I said I wasn't with Trudene," he inter-rupted. Suddenly he straightened, his thoughts focusing on his answer and upon the way Ma had spoken. "Ma . . . ?"

"Lige is wild about Trudene, son," Ma said.

"You mean it?"

"Yes, it's true. I don't want to cause you worry, but you're a stronger man than Lige. You can hold up under what I have to say. Trudene has taken care of Lige these past years . . . even come here days on end and helped us work. I should have told you when you first got back, but Lige didn't want me to. He loves you more than a brother. He was afraid you might be hurt."

"Good Lord!" Jake said. "No wonder Trudene seemed all shook up!"

"I guess she was scared of hurting you too," Ma said. "Or maybe she ain't real certain yet about which one of you Spaniard boys to pick. I talked to her about it. Told her she would have to make up her mind. She . . . well, she said it was Lige, that she couldn't ever let him go, but I don't know . . ."

"Sure it's Lige!" Jake said happily. "Why, confound it, this sure beats all! We'll throw a big old-time dance to celebrate! . . . They do want to get married, don't they, Ma?"

"Why, I reckon so." Ma's face looked puzzled. Her shrewd gray eyes studied Jake as he opened the barnyard gate. "Son, it never was like you to pretend things . . . not ever, in all your days."

"I'm not pretending! Trudene and Lige want each other, and I want Norma! I met Norma last night, and again today. She's the girl I want. She's grown up, and I know I love her, Ma. Why, everything will be just great from here on in!"

Ma spread her hands, then caught the front of

her apron and wiped her eyes. "And here I was," she choked, "thinking of having to tell you to go off and work somewhere else! It worried me sick, about the way you talked of developing our land and herds, of cutting and milling out all that big pine timber. I was worried because I knowed all the time that Lige was worried, and that I was going to have to tell you to let Trudene alone for your brother's sake. It's always hard, having to take sides about children, son. But like I say, you're strong, and in some ways Lige is weak."

"I understand how it is, Ma," Jake said. "But it's mostly Lige's nerves, is all. You stop your worrying right now."

Ma hurriedly followed Jake through the gate, then watched him chain it. She reached up to touch his chin, which was still swollen a bit and slightly blue from the blow inside the tavern.

"It ain't that I'm partial, son. But you're like your Pa was. You'll make out."

A thought struck Jake. He voiced it. "Ma, does Brack Mulvane have a lease on some of our timberland?"

Ma's smile faded. "Has he been here?"

Jake nodded, his face tense. "When he said he had a lease on that good pine timber, I called him a liar. Don't tell me I was wrong."

"He wasn't lying, son."

Jake said impatiently, "But why? Why did you and Lige lease that timberland? You know what I always wanted to do with that timber . . . cut it off, develop the swamps and slopes for cattle land."

Ma looked sadly across the fields where the heat-haze danced. "It was partly because of Lige and Trudene, son," she admitted. "I knowed if you had that fine timber to work with, you'd be around. And I knowed ... or thought I did, that you couldn't be around because of Trudene and Lige. I thought you'd just round up cattle and move up north. It's a sad thing to say, but that's about the way it happened ... that, and all the money old Mulvane offered us."

"Well, I know times were bad, Ma, and that you and Lige did need money. How much did Mulvane pay for the lease?"

"Five thousand dollars, cash."

"Five thousand? For that undeveloped strip?"

Ma nodded. "And the money did so many things for us, son."

"Well, I would reckon so, at that. Helped pay for more clearing, I guess, and for that new wagon and the big team."

"Oh, yes, and for so many more things that boosted all of Lige's dreams."

Jake stood thoughtfully, reins of the bay in hand. "I can't figure Mulvane paying out that much cash for the pine belt, then not even trying to develop it."

"No one could figure why he built that new road, either, just for a few big freight wagons that he operates between Skin Bayou, Sallisaw and Fort Smith."

"So Mulvane money built the new road I traveled on yesterday."

"That's right," Ma said. "And about the pine

belt, Jake; Mulvane told me he didn't want it developed, the timber cleared out or anything done to it. He said too much of the territory is being cut out. Said he wanted that belt to stay just like it is, maybe for future generations to enjoy . . . his own fifty kids and grandkids, he said, and laughed."

"Phooey! I can't figure Brack Mulvane thinking about future generations, even if they are his descendants from a dozen wives! He's got something else up his sleeve. And I'll find out what it is!"

"Brack Mulvane's dangerous, son," Ma said. "He keeps a dozen or more thugs around his places of business. I'm afraid of what he may do when his lease expires and you start cutting that timber."

Jake led the bay on under the barn roof and began to unsaddle. He glanced at Ma and grinned. "You're not too scared, though."

Ma looked at her son a long time, with pride welling up in her eyes. "You're just about right," she said. "I'm not much afraid of anything, now that you're back home and everything's going to be fine with the girl problem between you and Lige . . . When you planning to have that party . . . the big dance and all?"

"I don't see a thing wrong with tomorrow night."

"Jake, son, don't . . . well, don't let things get out of hand with whiskey."

"Aw, you know how those things go, Ma. If I barred whiskey, we couldn't have a party. Either that, or some of the wild bucks would slip it in anyhow. Tell you what we'll do, though. I'll just invite the boys that I think can handle their drinks pretty well."

Ma sighed. "Well, I'll go and fix the noon meal, and after that you better get started searchin' out the company you want. Them young bucks you used to know, why some of them scattered every which way and yon after the race for land in the Cherokee Strip was over, and they gambled off or sold their claims."

Ma started to turn away, then paused. "Jake, son, whatever you run up against here, I don't want you to ever kill anyone else."

Jake felt himself tense up, and swarming through his mind were faces with ghostly eyes . . . faces of men he had been forced to out-draw and kill.

"It has always been forced on me, Ma."

"I know. But there's something else I know, too, a thing I heard from your Pa one time after he came home from a whiskey peddling trip in Missouri. He knowed a gunman that wanted to stop his drastic way of life, and he figured out a way to distract enemies and squeeze his way out of trouble by using a powder rope."

"A what?"

"A powder rope . . . long strip of denim, with a lot of powerful powder rolled into it and the edges sewed up to hold it in. When a gunfight was right up against him and appeared unavoidable, he jerked that powder rope from the front of his shirt, struck a match and hurled it at his enemy. That way, the long blaze of burning powder allowed him time to avoid the trouble."

"Whew! Never heard of that."

"Maybe not ... But I'm gonna sew you up one, filled with that powder that was left over when you and Lige dug our new well a few years ago. I've kept it dry."

"All right. You fix one, Ma, and I'll wear it all the time."

CHAPTER NINE

Ma waited, watching him, and Jake stood beside the bay horse, thinking how in the span of a few short hours a man could pile up almost a lifetime of living. But the thought made him feel mighty good. Lordy, what all he had done in a night and a day! Two fights and two women, and the amazing discovery in the last one that was bound to shape and change his life. He pulled in a deep breath. Memory of Sabina Mulvane was very dim, unwanted, pushed aside or almost obscured by the thought of Norma.

Ma had said she was going to fix the noon meal, but still she kept watching him as he leaned back with his lean shoulder touching a post of the barn roof.

"Well, Ma, a fellow goes off wandering, and things change up," he said, turning philosophical and expansive with the happiness in him. He didn't like the thought of Mulvane's lease, but that would soon be done with. "It's in my mind right now to follow Lige out among the timber, no matter where he's tramping, and tell him about all the changes, but it might be a little embarrassing, for him and for me. So I'll tell you how we'll work it: I'll grain my horse while you fix something to eat, then I'll mount up and get to Sallisaw to advertise and promote our big dance and celebration. YOU can tell Lige I'm giving him and Trudene my blessing. Then have him go tell Trudene. Make it plain, just what it's all about."

He stopped briefly, grinning, then went on with growing exuberance: "I think I've got a pretty selfish reason for throwing this party, too. I want to advertise pretty damn quick that Norma Clifton is my girl, and that I don't want anybody else making passes at her, you see!"

Ma waved as she turned away. "Get on with you, Jake Spaniard!" she said.

A half-hour later, Jake was back astride the bay and turning into the road that led over the hummock and took off on its looping route to Sallisaw. He was thinking to return that night by way of the isolated tavern and pick up Norma when she got off from work.

He reached down and patted the neck of the bay horse. "You're plenty big enough to tote me and one mighty pretty little gal, ain't you, boy?" he drawled.

He would be timing things about right, he thought. Advertising a dance by word of mouth, especially when a man was choosy about the ones invited, could take up an almighty lot of time.

He was about a half mile along the road when a thought struck his mind. It was strange, but the old route winding through the forest reminded him of a road he had once traveled due south from Whiskey Smith, over in the Choctaw Nation, when thugs had forced a shootout at the Indian "pay town" of Skullyville. A feeling of impending danger, of being on the verge of enemy encirclement, wiped out the feeling of happiness he had known at home. He thought, "I wish I had brought along our old hog rifle." Take old Brack Mulvane, with some kind of nefarious plan up his sleeve, a man might need to do some distance shooting, Jake thought. But he rode on, touching the butt of his big cavalry pistol for reassurance. That cavalry pistol had a distance and a wallop almost like a cannonball. He kept an eye out for scattered herds of cattle as he traveled. Those Longhorn steers had recently been worth less than two bits a head, but now, up in Kansas, they were valuable. Jake hoped to recruit a crew and start a drive before wintertime.

The road was incredibly rough, evidently seldom traveled. The tracks of Lige's produce wagon were about the only ones he saw. He thought, "Old Brack Mulvane—if he has more money than brains, which I think he does—ought to build a road this way". But hell, though, there were only Arkansas-Oklahoma Indians—the fullbloods—past the old Spaniard homestead. No one gave a damn what kind of roads an Indian had to travel.

Jake's thoughts reached ahead to Sallisaw. He wondered what it would be like after three years away. But ten times three years wouldn't have changed it much, he reckoned. Then he thought of Lige's talk about strangers from the east coming in. Maybe Sallisaw had really grown. He started thinking about the men he knew in and near Pawnee too, and it was inevitable that he should remember Elmer Gordon. Now there was a man folks had marked, all right! Elmer Gordon had crawled right out of the muck along Big Skin Bayou, almost starved to death. But he had built himself a fortune, and his work had been similar to the things Jake planned. Elmer had cut the timber off the hummocks and drained the water off several hundred acres of worthless bogs along the stream by cutting a drainage ditch to the river. The fabulous production of that land when it was stirred out of its fallow mold had made local financial history. Elmer Gordon would have understood Jake's problem, and would have seen that he got the money for development. But from Brack Mulvane's talk, Elmer Gordon must be dead. Jake remembered the phaeton driver's derisive, mocking laugh and knew beyond the shadow of a doubt that Brack Mulvane or some of his thugs had played some dirty hand in Elmer Gordon's death.

Jake thought, "One of these days I'll visit the Gordon house and ask Elmer's wife Clarissa for the truth . . . if the thugs didn't do away with her too."

It was sad in more ways than one to think

about what might have happened to Elmer Gordon. He guessed he would have to contact others with money now—men like H. P. Kingman and C. T. Sloan, the two big bankers in town. Both bankers had been friendly and helpful to Pa at times in the past. Either bank should advance money to him, if he could just put his plans for development across to them.

He thought as he rode, "Maybe I'll kill two pelicans with one throw . . . spread word about the dance and talk to some big-money wizards too."

He entered the edge of town and wondered at once where in the world the boom was. The squalid slum settlements along the cracked brick streets looked worse than they had three years ago. The women and kids along the way looked just as sickly and desolate. They made up a hodgepodge of humanity standing or sitting outside cramped, rust-smeared sheet iron shanties or board and batten houses that had squatted here for fifty years. There were crooked and tilted little outhouses and clothesline poles between which a few ragged duds hung limply. It was a depressing sight, this city, and worse throughout the South since the ravages of the War, Jake guessed. Up north and in the Midwest, towns the size of Pawnee were cleaning up there slum areas, building new and better housing, planting beautiful trees and shrubbery, but not down here.

He slowed the bay, looking about him. Where in the hell was the boom? How did Ma and Lige manage to sell produce for any profit to such poor folks as were staring at him now? Then he topped a slight rise and saw the difference beyond the main business district. A whole row of fine new homes had sprung up. He guessed they were for the easterners that had come in and for the bankers and storekeepers and other prosperous town people. They were away from the squalor he had first seen. They were far away from the smelly, old restaurants and beer dives and the maws in the earth where miners had dug out coal to fire the boilers in the lumber mills. There always had to be differences like this, he thought . . . more prettiness than a man could dream for on the one hand, and squalor and filth on the other.

He was nearing the town's single, long main street, and bitter thoughts were hounding his mind when a huge cart drawn by a four-up hitch of oxen wheeled from a side street. The oxen were being goaded into a trot. At a glance, he noticed that the cart was loaded with sleek-fat Longhorn cattle. He slowed the bay, hearing the great beasts bawling out their crowded misery in the cart that looked almost as wide as a barn.

Jake thought the cart was going straight across the intersection, but he was wrong. He caught a glimpse of the driver's arms, heaving the lead oxen to the right, cutting sharply into Main Street. It was a wrong and tragic move for the load of cattle. Within an instant, disaster was right at hand. The cart was going too fast for the sharp turn, and one of the big wheels bounced across a corner of the curbing. Jake heard the cracking of bolted slats as the cart teetered sideward, throwing all the weight of the Longhorns to the left. The cart crashed over on its side with a harsh grinding against the bricks and cobbles, sending the lurching, bawling load of steers tumbling out.

Jake sent the bay to the curb and left it with trailing reins. He was leary, leaving the horse untied, but decided to trust it. Most of the dumped cattle were up and heading at a run down the street. Their massive heads were moving from side to side, their nostrils flaring. But one of the beasts was still down beside the wrecked cart, a pool of blood forming at its side where an iron tailgate rod had ripped its hide open from shoulder to flank. Jake walked nearer and saw that both the animal's front legs were broken. Blood ran from the steer's nostrils too, and one horn was totally gone. The huge beast was trying to get up, but its efforts were pitifully hopeless. Jake heard its breath coming in bellow-like snorts of pain and terror as he approached.

The driver of the cart had leaped to safety. Now he stepped up close and stood with his hands on his hips, looking down at the panting steer.

"You're lucky, fellow," Jake said. "Damned lucky."

The driver, naked from the waist up and brown and hairy as something just out of a jungle, merely glared at Jake and shrugged. He didn't say anything. He shuffled closer to the downed

Longhorn, and one of his muddy boots lashed out, its toe thudding against the steer's bloody nose.

"Stop that!" Jake commanded. "Don't you kick that animal again!"

The driver looked around, a sadistic pleasure shining in his pale glance.

"Whatsa mattah, frien'?" he sneered. "You som' kina squeamy-gutted panty wais', I guess."

Jake went at him, the heel of his hand catching the driver's shoulder, shoving him away. "You kick that brute again and you'll find out what I am! Stay back!"

The driver's belligerence melted right down into his naked paunch. Jake drew his cavalry pistol. He could hear a crowd gathering around him on the street and realized hundreds of eyes were watching him, including those of the dying steer. He took the beast out of its agony with one shot into its brain.

The crash of the gunshot had silenced the crowd, but now talk started again. When Jake looked around, he was amazed at the number of people. The disturbance had brought out everyone in town, it seemed. He held the smoking pistol a moment and looked the crowd over, searching for people he knew. Many of them were businessmen, clerks from the better stores, restaurant operators, bartenders, farmers and ranchers and a barber or two. But there near the curb was a group that made Jake's blood race. He recognized the Gibson boys, Ocie, Ken and the huge, muscle-bound Stapp. They were all good friends of the Spaniard family, and Jake knew by the way Ocie winked that they had recognized him. But it was their natures to just wait and see what happened, not saying or doing a thing. Jake grinned at them, letting them know he had seen them and was glad. He thought, "Why, right there in one spot is all the advertising I need for our dance." The Gibsons knew Jake's staunchest friends, and they could "know-rate" word to hell-and-gone in an hour.

A slow-cruising black phaeton began wheeling its way into the crowd. Jake stiffened, wondering if Brack Mulvane had nothing to do except push his nose into the affairs of others. He saw Rupe, the driver, pulling the phaeton up at the curb. A third man was in the phaeton now, and Jake recognized him: Thad Brill, the city marshal, who also was the town's chief of police. Brill got out of the rear seat of the phaeton and stood quietly, looking at the dead steer, then at Jake. Brill rolled himself a smoke.

A voice behind Jake, sharp and severe, said, "Spaniard, I want to know who gave you the authority to shoot and kill one of my best steers?"

Jake turned and saw one of the town's leading bankers, C. T. Sloan. Sloan was a heavy-jowled, middle-aged man who looked as if his face had never been exposed to the Oklahoma sun. His clothes were immaculate, his black shoes flashed.

Jake looked at him levelly and answered, "I just took the steer out of its misery, Mr. Sloan."

"You've tampered with my property!" Sloan

accused. "That steer came off my ranch, and was headed for the slaughter pens near town! If you had any sense, you would have gone for a good vet, or sent someone. A veterinarian could have saved that steer! And you stand there with a gun in your hand, just gawking!"

Jake holstered his still smoking pistol. "Take a closer look at that steer, Mr. Sloan. It's body is slit wide open, and its front legs smashed to bits, its head crushed. No one could have saved that steer."

The banker interrupted in a shrill voice, looking across at Brack Mulvane's halted phaeton and at Marshal Thad Brill, "I'll have you arrested, you stupid redneck!" He wheeled back to glare at Jake. "You're old Absalom Spaniard's boy, aren't you? . . . Brother of that idiot, Lige?"

Jake's face dipped at the banker like a beak of a jaundiced hawk. "Calling in the law is the only way you'd have guts enough to get at a Spaniard, you duck-footed bastard, you!"

The banker's lips twisted and his face turned pasty. He cringed backward, sucking in a slow, hard breath. Behind him, Jake heard Thad Brill's slow, deep voice. "Hand that gun back to me, butt 'wards me, and head out where my jail is, Spaniard! Start walkin'! . . . Go on, now, boy! I mean right now!"

CHAPTER TEN

The Sallisaw jail didn't show any more improvements than the town in general. Jake had been there before, several times after Lige had been slugged during the whiskey war, mostly because of fighting stirred up by Turk Munson. He hated the jail with a country-raised boy's innate hatred of confinement, and demanded a hearing or bond at once, but Thad Brill merely laughed.

"I allus like my company to cool their heels a spell," Brill drawled. "Makes me feel real bad when a prisoner rears up and declares he's just GOT to be gettin' on home . . . you know?"

Jake tried a bit of careful diplomacy. "This jail is not so bad, Marshal Brill. In fact, I was in it so often a few years back, it kind of looks and feels like home to me. I know you did your duty, the way you saw it, when you arrested me. But the thing I did was an act of mercy, just like you'd shoot a dog that was dying after being run over in the street."

"I don't waste powder and lead on a dog I figure is dying," Thad Brill said. He pulled his long-muzzled pistol and squinted down its glistening barrel. "I like to shoot something that's runnin', on its feet an' trying to get away from me . . . dog or man."

"Brill, I'd appreciate it if you'd get hold of the judge and let him set my bond. I'll be in position to do something good for you sometime."

"I've got my doubts about that," Brill said. "Never met a Spaniard yet that stirred up much of anything except trouble. Besides, I didn't like them hand signs you was makin' to the Gibson clan right after I took your gun."

"I was just motioning for them to take care of my horse," Jake said. "I'd just bought the horse, and it wasn't tied. I thought it might be stolen, or maybe get scared and run away."

Brill spat and holstered his pistol. He cocked his big boots on a table edge. "Ain't much of a likely story. I figure you was signalin' them Gibsons to break you out of jail here. That's the thing I've got in my mind, but I'll be ready for them, you can bet your life on that."

"Just what kind of charges will you bring against me, Brill?"

"That's up to Sloan," Brill said. "Maybe malicious assault, attack with a deadly weapon, or threatening or something like that. You know, you COULD spend a pretty good passel of time in this jail of mine . . . and our grub here is awful, when we have funds to buy any grub that is."

Jake stared at him, not liking the trend of the

marshal's talk. Thad Brill was a man of a para-doxical nature. On Sunday, he was a faithful church-goer, always listening avidly to the sermons and always throwing his portion of change into the old church till. But all the other days of the week, he walked the streets, swaggering with his big pistol strapped on. He sponged coffee at every restaurant, spoke only when spoken to, and that wasn't often, and his ferreting eyes searched out every corner of the town where he was born. Thad Brill was a confirmed killer, dreaded and feared, lord of all he surveyed in the community's confines. It was said he controlled the city court, and Jake guessed that was true.

"Who is the judge here now, Brill?" Jake queried.

The marshal shrugged. "You wouldn't know him. Jasper from up north somewhere, name of Uel Dillon. I figured we needed impartial judgment around here after the War was over, so I supported him. Besides, seemed like no one wanted the job. That's peculiar too, the town growin' an' all, but folks aren't carin' much about the law 'til they need it, like Sloan did awhile ago. About the only man interested in law an' order an' local politics is Brack Mulvane. I guess you remember him?"

Jake's temper got the best of him. "Won't ever forget that conniving old son-of-a-bitch!"

Thad Brill laughed.

Jake turned and sat down on a bunk. Automatically, he reached for the makings, but recalled that Brill had taken them. Oddly, though, the marshal had ignored the big kitchen matches. Jake took one from his pocket, chewed its stem a moment, then broke it between thumb and forefinger in his accustomed way. When he pitched the pieces into a corner, he saw a mouse pounce upon them just like they were bits of food. His face tightened. If a mouse in this crummy jail was THAT hungry, it was possible that prisoners were seldom fed either. Well, maybe fifty cents a day per prisoner would be allowed, with Thad Brill pocketing most of that and the prisoners getting occasional doles of soup and beans. A dull fury struck at Jake Spaniard, and he started thinking how many places in Oklahoma were ones of rare beauty and fairness. But this festering sore on the edge of his native country was not much better than a settlement full of renegades that you might have seen about thirty years ago during the Mexican War.

Marshal Brill turned and leaned back in a chair outside the bars. Time didn't mean anything to Brill. He wasn't sensitive enough to understand how a man behind bars could fret. Jake wondered what Ma and Lige would think when he didn't come home that night. He reckoned he didn't have anything in particular to worry about in the long run. Ma and Lige would eventually come in, as they always had, and Jake doubted that even Brill or Judge Dillon would have the audacity to stand up in the face of Ma's demands. Brill would like to keep Jake in jail for several days, so he could draw that board money. But Ma, with her game-fighting spirit, would not stand for that. So Jake reckoned that all he had to do was wait.

He was resigning himself to that when he heard footsteps hurrying across the floor of the courthouse corridor. He straightened, all at once alert. He knew he couldn't be mistaken. He had heard those same footsteps tapping before, going away from him across the floor inside that old hotel near the tavern. Sabina Mulvane was out there, coming toward the jail cell where he sat. She appeared almost at once; a big and imposing woman, dressed to perfection in a long, belted dress with a flowing, full skirt that ended just above her ankles. She wore high-heeled shoes that were a different color from the day before, and she stopped with them set wide apart, strong and uncompromising as she faced Marshal Brill.

"I saw everything that went on out there, Thad!" she said sharply. "When did you stoop to making a cheapskate arrest like that?"

She looked through the bars at Jake as she spoke, and her lips spread in a smile that belied the angry sound of her voice. Jake looked back at her, but didn't smile. He was noticing the way Thad Brill sat there, looking at Sabina's wide-legged stance as if there were an avid hunger in him that he couldn't contain. It wasn't a distant hunger, either, like that of a man who hopes but knows his hopes are useless.

Thad Brill was many things, but not much of a diplomat. He stood up. "Did Brack send you over here to badger me?" he said.

"I don't know what in the world you mean!"

"I think you do. Brack didn't object to me arrestin' Spaniard, when Sloan give me the nod. And I rode down to the disturbance with Brack."

"I don't know what you're getting at, and I don't know what you rode or did. All I know is that I'm going to put a stop to men being arrested for nothing. Open that cell door and let Jake Spaniard out of there!"

Brill looked at her. In his eyes was the dull hurt of a man coming out second best. The next instant his glance switched to Jake, and his hatred showed. "You want her to put up bond?" he demanded.

"No." Jake looked straight at Sabina Mulvane. "Thanks, but I'll make out."

She looked through the bars at him, her glance showing what some folks would have taken for a touching sympathy. But Jake's sharp mind, still filled with suspicion of those not his kind, fastened instantly on one possible reason for her visit here: Brack Mulvane was quick on the uptake, instantly conniving, always ready to pounce on anything that might be used to his advantage. Jake figured Mulvane had consented to having him jailed, then had sent Sabina here to pay him out. That way, Jake would feel obligated and thus be easier to deal with concerning that valuable belt of pines.

Jake continued to watch Sabina as she looked at him, and he thought of the strange ways of

98

women and the brazenness they could show. Suspicion warned him that her story about Mulvane wanting to be rid of her was too thin to smear. A woman as sharp as Sabina would not allow an old man to marry her, then cut her off without a cent. She could take old Brack Mulvane for half of what he was worth, or more.

Sabina was working again with her purse. "Please don't be so high and mighty, Mr. Spaniard. Let me help you."

He shook his head. "Ma and Lige will be in soon, if not them, then some of my friends. This little business isn't going to amount to anything."

Sabina finally sighed, then snapped her purse shut. Brill had resumed his seat. She stared angrily at him, then wheeled, flaunting her skirt against his face. Her high heels tapped determinedly down the corridor. Soon she was out of sight.

Brill's face was tinged with color, and his mouth was open slightly. Suddenly he stood up, hitching at his sagging gun belt.

"I don't think I get it, Spaniard. Not real good. You got something stashed out better than she's trying to hand to you?"

Jake didn't say anything. What he was thinking was special and secret . . . the memory of Norma Clifton, bringing alive a warmth and return of the vision of her, young and beautiful beyond all speaking.

Thad Brill turned and stamped along the corridor toward the outer office. It was quiet in the jail except for the unseen scurrying of rats and mice. Jake got up and paced the cell restlessly, wanting to tear out the bars with barehanded strength. It wasn't so much the thought of his immediate predicament, but he knew what gossip could do to his plans. He had come home, hoping to be respected and looked up to as a progressive man of affairs. He didn't want folks thinking of him as a brawling, rough and tough scrapper from the backwoods, as they had thought of Pa. But that was the way it would be. People all over town would be saying that Old Ab Spaniard's son, the big one that looked almost exactly like him, was back home after three years, and already he's in jail on account of breaking the law. Jake thought of the bankers, Sloan and Kingman, and knew that his hopes of borrowing from anyone in or near Sallisaw had gone right down the drain. He couldn't raise money to get out that valuable timber or to gather a riding crew to round up a northbound herd. Banker Sloan would see to that, even if he didn't bring charges against Jake for shooting that helpless steer.

Jake was still pacing his cell a few minutes later when the three Gibson boys traipsed in, followed dourly by Thad Brill. The Gibson boys stopped at Jake's cell and grinned in at him, as if they were playing a big joke on someone. Then from their pockets they pulled out wads of greenbacks and handed them to Brill for his bond. Brill opened the cell door and soon Jake was free and out on the street with the Gibson boys, telling them about the forthcoming dance and how he would like for them to spread the news.

"Pick the bucks that can hold their drinks if you can," he said, shaking hands with them, warmed by their backwoodsy friendliness. "Ma's hard against fighting and drinking ... And I'll pay back that bond money, sooner than soon."

The Gibson boys nodded, looked at each other and grinned but didn't say anything. They climbed into the saddles of horses tied at the curb near Jake's mount, then suddenly both gobbled like wild turkeys and raced away ....

CHAPTER ELEVEN

It had been a swift thing, without Thad Brill showing his usual harsh reluctance to let Jake go. After the marshal's earlier adamant attitude, his tempered actions had seemed puzzling. But Jake had wanted out of that stinking jail, and he didn't figure he had to question motives of either Brill or the Gibson boys.

He walked along the street with lifted face and squared shoulders. The late-afternoon sun felt clean and pleasant after the stench of the jail's interior. The marshal hadn't objected at all when he had requested his pistol and now the gun rested heavy, smooth and snugly against his hip. He had deliberately walked past his horse and was almost a block from the jail before he became aware that people on the sidewalk were stopping and turning to stare at him. Then he saw businessmen and store clerks edge out to the front doors of their establishments. They were watching him. His keen, coppery eyes studied them, and at first he was puzzled, then he became aware that he was walking the gamut of resentful and hostile stares.

He was a Coke Hill native, owner of Indian land, and here he had come back to cause trouble just like old Absalom Spaniard had done. He sensed that the people of this town hated him, not only because of his ownership of land, but because of his Indian heritage. It was a different and definite hatred, more intense than in the old days, and he knew why. He had stood and ridden proud and tall in the Confederate cavalry. He was walking proudly now. He wasn't staying in the accustomed, stoop-faced Indian role. He was tramping the streets of this old town like the sidewalks and the buildings had been made for him as well as for the wealthiest one of them, and they couldn't stand it. He was breaking all the rules of a set society which relegated all Arkansas-Oklahoma Indians as members of the country swamp rats. To the people watching, it was galling. He knew just how it was, and he relished the knowledge of their thinking.

His head tilted higher, and it didn't show on his face, but there was anger in him. He was thinking how ordinary, decent folks like those staring at him could feel hatred for someone like themselves and then tolerate, even look up to someone like Brack Mulvane, who had made his pile of money by using every crooked tactic in the book, including cattle thieving and whiskey smuggling. People here didn't think of Brack Mulvane's rotten roles in politics, his activities during the wholesale whiskey war, or of any of his gambling and racketeering where he had accumulated his pile of cash. Folks didn't look upon Brack Mulvane as a menace to society. He owned a fine home, fancy phaetons and a riding stable or two for visiting dignitaries down from the Oklahoma City capital. No one stopped to think how Brack Mulvane had come by the fortune he had made.

That was the way it went . . .

It could have been the trend of his thoughts, the bitterness, that made Jake Spaniard want to test the thing out to its fullest. Whatever it was, when he saw old H. P. Kingman looking out through the plate glass front of his bank, Jake turned with the sudden grace of a drill sergeant, pushed open the door of the bank and went in.

"Howdy, Mister Kingman," he said.

Kingman looked at him with heavy-lidded eyes. "What is it you want here, Spaniard?"

"I just dropped in for a talk, if you have time."

Kingman's heavy-lidded stare intensified. "You got home broke, I guess. That seems to be a common affliction among your kind."

Jake looked steadily back at him, knowing the banker's animosity was too thick to penetrate with words of explanation, about Sloan's steer or anything else. But he damned well wasn't going to let Kingman's remark just rest.

"Give me a quick definition of 'my kind,' banker," he said.

Kingman seemed temporarily taken aback. Probably it was because Jake Spaniard wasn't

104

talking with the drawl, the backwoods slang of previous years.

Then the banker said flatly, "If you've got sense enough to ask a question like that, you know what I mean. Most of the people that come out of the backlands of the region are moonshiners, drunkards . . ."

Jake's face dipped forward. "The little moonshining done by Indians couldn't hold a light to what I've seen among the big racketeers who run distilleries as large as the U.S. government," he said.

"Those things were forced out by Federal edicts, years ago."

"Were they? Who can prove it? How many Federal officers patrol the deep woods of the country now?"

Kingman's face stilled. "You're trying to cover up the real issue. Territory Indians were always like slinking cats. You can't change a bobcat's spots. Country people are as bad as the damned people out here at the edge of town. They won't do anything to clean up or get better housing."

Jake's teeth showed solid and strong between flattened lips.

"Several people I used to know once tried to borrow money here to improve their farms and ranches. You have millions, but you wouldn't advance them a cent."

"I'm handling money of depositors! None of those people made good risks."

"I'm a good risk," Jake said. "My old Pap always had the reputation of paying his debts.

So do I. So does Ma and Lige. And the Confederate Army that protected you here thought I was plenty important enough to trust with some mighty big things. I'm just handing this to you for the record. Now I want to borrow some money from you, and it's a solid investment . . .a fortune in virgin pine timber on the land we own."

Kingman lifted a restraining hand. "And what else? I've heard rumors of how some men beat the truth out of Lige. That you're planning a cattle drive to Kansas City or to the railheads north. And wooden bridges across the swamps to support wagons to haul your timber! I think you're a crazy man."

Jake pulled in a deep breath. "Things sure get around. I won't ever write any letters about private affairs again."

"Nothing's private, Spaniard. You're laboring under a misconception. Not very much in the Oklahoma Territory is private anymore. Girls talk and mothers talk. That's the way it is."

Jake wheeled and went outside. His lips were set and twin rings of fury edged them. He had verified what he had suspected in the jail. He was exceptionally disappointed because there was Norma. He wanted to marry her. He wanted to get married and start some progressive work. He wanted to do good here on the land where he was born and raised. A large sign directly ahead intensified the bitterness in him. The sign dominated the view along the street. It read: Brack Mulvane Enterprises, Inc. That was all, but the sign was so big it hinted that Mulvane Enterprises, could cover a host of things.

Jake was looking the place over when Mulvane stepped outside and confronted him. He stopped, watching him, then glanced around through the window and saw the vague profile of Rupe. Brack Mulvane was not alone. He had backing, and he would always have backing as long as he appeared in public, Jake knew. Mulvane was smiling, but evidently, he had more sense than to offer his hand to Jake Spaniard for the second time that day.

"I've just got news of something that does me good, Spaniard," Mulvane said without preliminaries. "That stepson of mine came in awhile ago, black and blue all over. I made him tell me what happened. Maybe it'll tone down his rapacious urges for a little while, at least. I want to thank you for beating hell out of him."

Jake didn't say anything. He merely shrugged and started on.

Mulvane's urgent voice stopped him. "I've got a good proposition for you, Spaniard, if you'll listen. It's possible I could raise some money for you, for timber and swamp development you're planning, if you handle it like I say."

"You think I'd trust you in a partnership?"

"I'm not asking that," Mulvane said. "I'll loan money for worthy activities. All I would ask is that you leave certain portions of that heavy timber untouched, for posterity."

"Hell!" Jake laughed. "Posterity! . . . That's a hell of a word coming from you!"

Mulvane's eyes flashed dangerously. "I dare you to meet me in the timber near the Pawnee, say day after tomorrow. I'll show you what I mean and just why I'm interested."

Jake looked at him narrowly. "I can't figure out any reason to meet you anywhere, Mulvane. Your conniving brain is probably fixing up some trick."

Mulvane said tauntingly, "You're not *afraid* to meet me to discuss business, are you, Spaniard? Your ol' Pa never was afraid to meet me anywhere."

A sharp perception materialized in Jake's eyes. "I'll meet you at the *edge* of our timberlands, and you be alone . . . And I'll tell you something else, Mulvane: Someone will know where I've gone and just who I'm going to meet, just in case you have some of your maulers there in the brush ahead of us."

Mulvane smiled and lit up a large cigar. "You don't trust me at all, but it's a deal. We'll meet on the road south of the tavern and go to the edge of the big timber from there. Is that all right?"

Jake nodded and left him, wondering just what sort of deal Mulvane had up his sleeve. Then a thought occurred to him. If anyone would know, it might be Norma Clifton. A person never could tell what a waitress in such a place as the old tavern might hear . . . some gossip let slip by a drunk, or the remark of a lounger. Besides, he wanted to see her anyhow. He had already planned on it.

He glanced at the lowering sun as he reached the bay horse and mounted. Summer days were so long, it would be three hours or more before dark, but he could wait at the tavern until she came in. He circled the block and headed out of town.

"Shucks, I'll just stick to my first thought too," he murmured. "I'll hang around the tavern and hotel until Norma finishes her work for the night, then take her home."

As he struck the main road, some impelling urge made him turn in the saddle and look back. It was odd, but unease crowded in on his excitement about seeing Norma. It made him wonder. He had the feeling that hidden eyes were watching him, maybe to see which turn in the road he would take. He was surprised at how clearly the full length of Main Street stood out. He saw people moving and others just standing, looking in his direction. Brack Mulvane was plainer than all the others in the latter groups. Jake guessed it was because of the whiteness of his shirt and the sweep of his black string tie. Mulvane was in the same place where Jake had left him. Mulvane was plainly watching intently as he rode on.

Elmer Gordon's red brick house, just off the road leading out of town, looked about the same as it had three years before. Jake took into account again Mulvane's statement that Elmer Gordon was dead, but Elmer's wife Clarissa had probably not moved. A couple of hacks with teams tied at hitching rails stood in front. He guessed that Clarissa had company. The warmth of old memories came alive in him as he looked at the big house in its grove of pines. Jake Spaniard had always been welcome there as a youngster. Wealth had never gone to Elmer Gordon's head.

He was riding along with his mind caught up in introspection when he heard the fast grind of wheels and the hoofbeats of a trotting horse behind him.

He glanced back and saw a sleek black pony pulling a new red-wheeled buggy with trimmings of glistening steel. The buggy pulled swiftly up beside him. Sabina Mulvane was on the seat alone, her slender hands gripping the checklines, her glance fastened upon Jake.

"Pull over," she called. "I've got to talk to you!"

"What about?"

She motioned toward the side of the road. "Stop, Jake! Please! It's important . . . something you need to know."

He pulled the bay over and stopped, and she eased the buggy up beside him. He knew, even at that, they were taking up too much of the narrow road, but she didn't seem to give it a thought. He looked at her sharply and knew why. Sabina Mulvane was drunk. Not wobbly drunk nor maudlin drunk, but drunk in the quiet, exuberant way of one who knew just how much alcohol it took to reach that certain stage of intoxication.

"What is it?" he asked impatiently.

She gestured ahead toward a curve in the road.

Her eyes shone with an animal excitement boosted by alcohol. "Follow me, Jake. A forest road to our country place. We'll talk there."

"No dice," he said harshly, and his pressing boots sent the bay into a gravel-scattering lope.

"Wait, Jake! You've got to go with me!" she shouted. "I have things to tell you that will affect you entire life!"

He ignored her, knowing that only one thing could come out of her drunken state. But almost instantly the careening buggy was up beside him. He noticed the convulsed look on Sabina's face.

"Jake, you've got to go talk with me! You've got to listen to what I have to say!"

"Tell me now . . . fast," he said, checking his horse.

"Jake, you know we can't talk here for any length of time! I tell you, it's important that we discuss something! . . . Jake, you were right in the hotel room, when you said I was fronting for my husband, trying to buy the timber and land that he couldn't buy from you. But not now! I have to cut out from him, Jake, for good this time! And I've learned things you need to know!"

"What's making you cut loose from Mulvane now?"

Her face looked angry and resentful as she leaned toward him. "Brack was enraged because I didn't get the thing done that he wanted done. He accused me of weakening . . . . told me go, get out . . ."

"You expect me to believe that tripe?"

Her eyes suddenly shadowed. "All right," she said. "Someday you'll remember I tried to tell you everything! But you don't know what it is to feel appreciated, do you? Like for the way I paid you out of jail?"

He said evenly, "The Gibson boys did that."

"Oh, yes!" She laughed scathingly. "They were out front, all right, hitching at their pants and spitting and doing nothing ... not a thing for you. *I* was the one that put up the money to get you out of there! If you don't believe it, talk to the Gibson boys and find out!"

Jake looked at her, and once again a feeling of unease clawed through him. Too much attention was being focused upon him. He had the feeling a conspiracy was brewing against him in Sallisaw, something worse than he had ever thought. He wondered if Sabina was lying. Then, remembering the way the Gibson boys had acted, grinning and mysterious, he thought at least that much of Sabina's talk measured up to the truth. He motioned her on, knowing he owed it to himself and to Ma and Lige, to find out as much as possible. Even if he found out Sabina was lying, that would be some advancement in the problems that were confronting the family, he thought. Besides, you never could tell about a woman. Maybe she really was through with Mulvane for good ....

Jake saw the flash of her smile as she nodded and the buggy wheeled ahead. The flashing red wheels of the new vehicle made a striking contrast against the green of the pines. Sabina turned the buggy off to the right on a side road and Jake followed it, his copper-tinted eyes questing for danger at each shadowed turn. Finally, he saw a huge lodge of logs and chinking beyond a circular drive. Twin chimneys graced either end, and a long porch invited entry. To the left, shining between a trellis banked with red roses, he caught a glimpse of a lake. He thought, "Well, the Mulvanes sure have it rich . . ."

Sabina halted the buggy in front of the lodge with amazing dexterity for her drunken state and came to earth. Jake dismounted, trusting the bay, and left the horse with trailing reins.

CHAPTER TWELVE

If she had been a woman of lesser beauty, the brazen way she spun to face him, stretching and flinging her arms up, might have repelled Jake Spaniard. Even as it was, something about her faintly irked him, as if he had been pulled unwillingly into a feminine trap. But his distaste was overshadowed and conquered by the pure animal appeal of her. One thing a man could say about Sabina Mulvane, she was all woman. Every curve of her body under that blue taffeta dress was feminine and appealing, drawing and holding his gaze like a magnet despite his efforts to pull his eyes away.

She turned from him and started up the steps of the porch. "Come in, Jake. I'll fix you up a drink."

"Thanks, but I don't need a drink," he said. "We can sit on the porch and talk."

She turned her head and looked at him over her shoulder. "Aw, Jake, don't be a prude! Go around the lodge, then, and have a seat behind the trellis while I fix up something to drink. I know you're not in such a hurry that you can't spend a leisurely five minutes with me."

Impatience was riding him, but he realized that arguing with her would only prolong this thing. He nodded agreement and went around the notched logs of the lodge, conscious that she was watching him before she opened a door and went inside.

Jake didn't find chairs behind the trellis, but Sabina rushed out with them almost at once. She set them close together, then laughed and went back inside the lodge. When she came out again she was wearing a checkered print dress with buttons all the way down the front. She held two glasses filled with amber liquid, and as she handed one of them to Jake, she asked, "You like the dress, Jake?"

"It's all right." He took a chair and held his whiskey.

She sat down on the grass in front of him, and for the first time he noticed she was barefooted. She drew her legs sideward under her and looked at him coyly. She must have slipped a long drink inside the lodge, Jake thought. Her eyes had that wild, frantic whiskey shine. He downed his drink swifty, wanting to get down to the business of their talk.

"You said you had things to tell me," he said.

"Yes ... Jake, I suppose you realize by now that the big belt of pines you and your folks own is very valuable to my husband ... or ex-husband if you want to call him that, because I don't intend to live with him anymore."

"What is it . . . a treasure hoard or something in that forest? I can't imagine it being as valuable as all that to a man who is already rich."

She sipped her drink and looked at Jake obliquely. "It's something without which Mister Brack Mulvane's financial world would tumble about his ears," she said. "And he knows it, and doesn't intend to rest until that land's his own."

"All right. Did you bring me here to explain it all or not?"

Sabina laughed, killed her drink and sent the glass rolling across the grass.

"No, I'm not going to just tell you. I'm going to take you right into those piney woods and show you . . . but when this deal is over, I want my split."

"What kind of split?"

"Oh, a few thousand. But that won't hurt you, and I'll get out of the country . . . after you and I have been together for a while."

His gaze narrowed upon her. He didn't say anything.

She looked back at him, her eyes filled with a strange brilliance. "Jake, no man ever moved me the way you do."

"We were talking about property that Mulvane wants," he said.

She ruffled her golden hair and suddenly stood erect. She looked at him an instant with that whiskey-wildness in her eyes, then began to lift her arms and whirl around in a barefooted, drunken and weaving dance. Jake Spaniard left the chair and started across the lawn. But she wasn't too drunk to notice. She stopped dancing and made a catlike leap, catching both his arms as she blocked his way. She pushed her face almost against his and began to scream. She kept it up until he thought she had blown her brains with alcohol. Then he reached and pressed a hand over her mouth and said heatedly, "You shut that up! I've had all I can take of this! You hear me? You scream at me that way again and I'm liable to wring your neck!"

The whinny of the bay warned him, but not quite soon enough. Brack Mulvane's voice said at the near corner of the lodge:

"Don't panic and rush off, Spaniard."

Jake froze, half expecting a bullet, but then he saw that Mulvane didn't even have a gun in his hand.

"You did a wonderful job," Mulvane said to Sabina. "No man would have been listening for our rig coming up over the pine needles with you putting on a show like that."

The word "our" got across to Spaniard, and his glance swiveled slightly. He saw the dark form of Rupe through the rose trellis. Rupe had a sawed-off shotgun in his hands.

Sabina faced Mulvane and said in a cutting voice, "You said you'd give me two hours, Brack. You and Rupe were going to wait on the old creek road near the tavern."

Mulvane's dark glance flicked at her. "We weren't too sure of you, darling."

117

"Maybe it doesn't pay you to be too certain of me!" she flared. "Hard cash and fancy clothes . . . sometimes they aren't enough!"

She moved close to Jake, teetering slightly on bare feet as she let her hand trail against his cheek. She wheeled and entered the rear door of the lodge. Rupe, still holding the shotgun levelled, came around the trellis where the roses bloomed. Rupe's lips were wet, and globules of sweat shone on his brow. "Boss, I'd kill a woman of mine for saying something like that!"

Mulvane shrugged. "I've had my share of women in that way, Rupe. All I want from any woman now is the help she can give at times. It's a thing . . ."

Jake interrupted bluntly, "What kind of frame-up is this?"

Mulvane took off his wide straw hat and ran his fingers around its sweaty band. "Frame-up's an ugly word, Spaniard. Let's just call it a move of self-protection on my part. You caused it yourself. I offered to meet you in the big pine country and show you what I have there, but you said you were going to tell someone where you were going, beforehand, and I couldn't tolerate that."

Rupe stepped closer, the sawed-off muzzle of the shotgun almost pointing straight at his guts. Mulvane went on in his suave voice, "You don't have anything to get excited about if you do what I say, Jake. I just didn't want you to let others know you were going to meet me. In case you DIDN'T cooperate, and I had to take . . . steps."

"Stop beating around the bush, Mulvane! If you've got something on my land, I want to see it. Let's get the move on."

"Fine. That's what I call a man ... Now we're gonna let you ride your horse. But you'll be directly in front of the hack we came here in, and I'll drive while Rupe holds the shotgun. We'll tell you which way to turn. You pull a fast one, and Rupe's gonna blast a hole in your back big enough to throw a hound through. You understand?"

"You make it pretty clear, Mulvane. I'm ready, anytime."

"All right." Mulvane gestured around the lodge. "Lead out."

Jake stepped around the trellis, wondering briefly why they hadn't taken his gun. But they felt secure with Rupe holding the shotgun at his back, he reckoned. That was what *THEY* thought ... Spaniard had the urge to laugh. No matter how fast Jake Spaniard drew, whirled and triggered his pistol, he would be dead on his feet from a shotgun blast before he could get the first move made ... That was what *THEY* thought, Jake knew.

He passed their halted hack, which had rolled up quietly. He reached his bay horse and mounted.

"Turn right and follow the old forest road," Mulvane ordered. "We'll be right behind you ... and damned close!"

They turned onto a dim, old wagon road or Indian trail that followed hummocks of land for an

119

interminable time through the forest. The pines on either side soared to tremendous heights. Now and then they spooked big herds of wild Longhorn cattle. They penetrated the forest farther than Jake had ever gone.

Jake pondered further, why they hadn't even tried to take his gun. But then, on a sudden double take, he figured it out: Old Brack Mulvane would want to tell his associates that Jake Spaniard, notoriously swift with a pistol, had been forced into the forest with his gun still on him and had made no attempt to draw. Actually, Jake Spaniard knew in his mind and heart, he could leap from his mount, jerk his pistol and kill both of them. Rupe had always been a bumbler. He would fire and miss . . . But then how would Jake ever know their woodland plans?

Once they crossed a slough on a flat-bottomed ferry operated by a very old man in patched trousers who looked like he hadn't shaved in twenty years. As they went deeper and deeper into the forest, another thought occurred to him about the big pistol he had been allowed to keep. Maybe the shrewd Mulvane wanted Jake to have the consolation of the gun, perhaps hoping he would make a try for it and they could get rid of him for keeps. The thought had first taken dim shape in his mind when they had crossed on the ferry, and the bearded old duffer had looked at his gun, then back at Mulvane and Rupe and winked. A man had to change thoughts with the turn of events or the things he observed, Jake knew.

Jake didn't put anything past Brack Mulvane, not even premeditated murder. And when a fellow got right down to cases, Jake had been seen with Mulvane's young wife, and Rupe could swear to it. That wasn't good ... Jake Spaniard figured he was caught up mighty close, in more ways than one, because he felt compelled to see what Mulvane had going deep among the pines.

The road had gradually circled, and sundown was on the left. A golden streak of brilliance reflected in a tributary of the creek. In the distance, winging over the channel of the stream, Jake saw a blue heron. Gauging his position, he realized that even after all the driving Mulvane had done, holding to the dry hummocks, the old tavern and hotel in the backwoods were not over five or six miles away as a straight-flying bird would wing. That was small comfort, though. A man would have a hell of a time finding his way through this dense forest at nighttime, either riding or walking. Mulvane had ordered too many twists and turns.

Yep, a man had to play his hand according to how the cards fell, and only a stubborn fool would refuse to change his mind. Jake Spaniard was beginning to feel with a growing certainty that Mulvane and Rupe, and no telling how many others, intended to get rid of him. Jake even began to conjecture a massive ambush set up for him around just about every turn.

Twilight came quickly after the sun had gone. He rode up a muddy slope, aware that the hack was right behind. The slope crossed a small tract of grazing land, then again entered the timber. Jake found himself riding under a solid canopy of foliage among some of the finest timber he had ever seen.

He tensed in his saddle as the slope dropped off into a deep and narrow canyon and he heard the bawling of cattle directly ahead. A cattle-rustler stronghold, he thought. No wonder old Mulvane didn't want timber cut away to reveal his rustling operations. Then suddenly something else jolted into Spaniard's mind. A smell he couldn't mistake penetrated through the night mist. He knew instantly what Mulvane had brought him here to see.

"Get off your horse and tie it," Mulvane ordered. "Then start walking, straight ahead."

Jake obeyed, and almost in the same instant saw the glow of many fires reflected in the water of a creek he figured was Black Fox. Shadowy figures of many men moved to and fro, and scores of giant barrels stood everywhere. Here, where the edicts of Federal law prohibited it, was one of the biggest moonshine whiskey operations in the United States.

Jake knew the purpose of the new road and the many side roads through the uplands. Old Mulvane had hired them built to easily drive herds of stolen cattle to Indian Territory or Whiskey Smith sale rings. And Mulvane's huge wagons with false bottoms hauled whiskey to the outside world by the barrels.

Mulvane and his hirelings . . . the strangers

Jake had first seen inside the tavern...had done away with all the old methods that Pa had used years ago. The old single-drum outfits, with worms inside cooling barrels and lead lines from cooking mash would have looked puny compared to this streamlined operation. Tremendous vats of copper held the mash, and copper worms and cooling systems were used throughout. High atop the tall trees an impenetrable brush arbor had been constructed to spread and diminish the smoke from the cooker fires. The only thing Brack Mulvane had not been able to suppress was the smell. Mash and whiskey and even the pot tails had a smell that was bound to come out.

No wonder Brack Mulvane hadn't wanted this vast forest to be cut over for lumber. Timber work and development of the piney belt would have revealed one of the largest illegal whiskey operations in the world.

"Go on down and meet the crew," Mulvane ordered, and Jake stepped forward, looking keenly around him as he walked.

He saw several men lounging on blankets and cots and burlap bags, watching the thin pencil lines of raw whiskey that poured into crocks and kegs from the copper lines.

The string of drums, under which the subdued fires twinkled, seemed to reach into infinity along the bank of the stream. They looked ghostly, like dancing fire devils in the night. At least a hundred barrels of mash were inside those cookers, Jake thought. There were probably another fifty barrels already fermented and ready to pour in over the pot tails to start a new "run" when this one was made. The magnitude of the operation appalled him. He even conjectured that Brack Mulvane shipped out loads of whiskey by boat down the stream that eventually reached the Arkansas and Mississippi rivers and thus on out to sea . . .

A thick-chested man, shaggy headed and darkly clothed came around one of the big cookers and stopped. Jake recognized him. It was the tough man who had hurled the beer mug that had struck Jake inside the tavern. The man recognized Jake and his eyes suddenly gleamed with animosity. He watched Jake without saying anything, and Jake watched him. Finally Brack Mulvane gestured to Jake and said to the man, "Meet Jake Spaniard . . . my prospective partner."

"We've met," the man said. That was all he said. He sat down on a burlap sack and remained there, silently watching the fires under the cookers and the little ropes of "white lightning" that flowed into the jugs.

"This is my top man here," Mulvane said about the man. "He can run off more whiskey from less mash than any man around Sallisaw, almost as good a turnout as your Pa used to get."

"Before the whiskey trouble," Jake said, and his voice was an ominous rumble deep in his throat. Then he added, "How long have you been operating this illegal distillery outfit on our land . . . on Spaniard land?"

"Right after I got the lease from your Ma and Lige," Mulvane said.

Jake was aware that Rupe was close behind him with that sawed-off shotgun, and that all those rough characters were watching him. It was time to do some acting, Jake thought, and unease crowded through him, because he had never been one to revert to pretense. But he sure better do a good job of pretense now, he thought.

"It's a neat and interesting setup," he said to Mulvane. "Why, a deal like this ought to bring in more dough than the lumber from five hundred acres of good pines . . . looking at it from a long-range viewpoint, that is."

"I'm glad you can see it that way," Mulvane said. He lit a fresh cigar. "It's a thing your Pa would have grasped pretty quick. And you're a lot like your Pa was, Jake. I can see it, and I've been banking on it. I can use a man like you in this business."

Jake sauntered along the row of copper cookers. Mulvane and Rupe followed him. He went the whole distance to the last drums and cookers, then turned back, facing Mulvane squarely.

"Just what part do you expect to have me play in this racket?"

Mulvane didn't hesitate. "I first wanted to buy the big pine grove for a hiding place, but in view of the plans you've already written to your family about . . . and the fact that you've now seen what's going on here . . . gives me another idea. You could actually start working out the timber, in a small way, and rounding up some cattle to drive north too, without bringing riders here deep in the pine country. This is about the only good place left in the region large enough to thoroughly hide a distillery operation of this size."

"And you would call that a partnership?" Jake asked, jeering him.

"Sure. What would you call a partnership?"

Jake said with continuing pretense. "A half share in this whole operation. That's what I'm demanding! Hell, you talk about me cutting a little timber, and driving a few wild cattle, but you've got a fortune here!"

Brack Mulvane looked at Jake a long time. The fires under the cookers made their constant crackle and pop. Darkness beyond the firelight closed in quickly.

"You know better than to demand such a thing," Brack Mulvane finally said. "What could you do to earn a partnership like that?"

Jake deliberately showed a smirk. "I could keep my mouth shut around Federal officers ... many of them good friends I've known for years."

Mulvane's eyes slitted, almost flashing sparks in the firelight.

"You won't be talking to Federal officers anyhow," he said.

"You got any guarantee of that?" Jake asked.

Mulvane glanced around at the faces of his henchmen, including Rupe. "The minute you start talking to Federal officers, something bad is going to happen to your Ma and Lige . . . and maybe to that little Clifton girl I hear you've taken to so quickly. Turk Munson told me all about that."

Jake started walking again, saying to Rupe as he passed him, "Your hands getting tired holding that shotgun, man?" Apparently there was a vast nonchalance on Jake, but all of it was wholly feigned. "Threats never scared a Spaniard, Mulvane," he said.

Mulvane laughed. "Threats scared your half-wit brother, Lige. Once he got pretty close here, him and that loud mouthed hound, and a couple of my boys collared him . . . Lige never showed up again."

"Lige lost some of his nerve after getting bashed up in that old whiskey war," Jake said, controlling his sudden fury. "I'm talking about any strong and healthy Spaniard of the name . . . " He let his voice trail off and wheeled around so swiftly he heard Rupe's shotgun cock. "Look, Mulvane, I see you've got a good thing here. I want a substantial piece of it. There are plenty of things I can do, like selling the whiskey towns or making contacts. I've learned plenty of things to help. Old Whiskey Smith was my hangout before Mexico."

Mulvane said adamantly, "Your price is too damned steep."

Jake sat down near one of the cookers, leaning forward to smell the fumes from the crock under the cooler spout. "Say, why don't we have a few drinks of this stuff?" he asked.

"Sure," Mulvane said. He gestured to the bearded man. "Get the man a fruit jar. Let him dip himself a swig."

The man got up with a growl, very reluctantly, and moved away to some wooden cases. He returned with a quart jar and glumly handed it to Jake Spaniard. Jake rose, stepped forward and dipped some whiskey from the crock closest to him. He took a sip. He grimaced and spat it out.

"That's practically backings." He looked down the line of cookers. "Where's some of the first cook off?"

"Backings, hell!" the rough man muttered. "It's all alike. We don't start one cooker at a time here. And the liquor didn't start until less than an hour ago."

Jake tasted again and feigned a gag. He looked at Mulvane and Rupe. "If this stuff is from the first cook off, then you're puking the mash. Too much heat. You're going to have to cut some fire."

"Hell," the man said again, but he was concerned. He got up and started to reach for the jar in Jake's hand. "Gimme that."

Jake dumped the contents of the jar contemptuously back into the crock and looked down the line of fires . . . If he could just get to that farthest one, there near the wall of timber . . . He headed toward it, carrying the jar. Mulvane and Rupe were close upon his heels. They stopped near him as Jake stooped over the last crock and leaned down to dip up the whiskey. The others were several paces away. Now was the time, Jake thought. He smiled up at Mulvane and Rupe as he let the jar gurgle in the whiskey. They stood close to the fire under the cooking drum, the flames lighting their faces plainly. Jake straightened up, still smiling, and tilted the almost full jar to his lips.

He actually took a long drink, thinking ahead and deliberately fortifying himself for what he knew he might have to go through. He remembered Ma's words, too, when she had sewn the powder in the long rope of denim which he kept tucked inside his shirt.

"Whew!" he said appreciatively to Mulvane, and lowered the jar from his lips. "No mash pukings in this . . . Look at the fire there. Not half as high as the rest."

He said it so casually that Mulvane and the others couldn't resist looking. At that instant Jake hurled the jar at Mulvane's head, then jerked the rope of powder from his shirt front and cracked it out at full length like a bullwhip, directly into the flames of the first two fires. A boom and a massive burst of flames soared up like a high and firey wall between Jake and his enemies. He leaped away from the last huge copper drum that was blown off its rock base and plunged headlong into the shelter of the trees. He heard the roar of Rupe's shotgun. Pellets of buckshot whistled through the leaves overhead and pinged off the bark of the trees.

"Get him, men!" Brack Mulvane shouted.

129

"Damnit, don't let him get away!"

Jake raced into a thicker clump of timber, tripping and falling several times over tangled vines. Always, he struggled to his feet and glanced back before racing on. He saw shadowy figures of men in hot pursuit. Pistols and shotguns in their hands continued to roar, and Jake thought, "Damnation! They keep hurling that much lead and I'm almost certain to get hit sooner or later, even by accident."

CHAPTER THIRTEEN

He was aware of an almost overwhelming urge to stop, jerk his own pistol and down some of his pursuers, but he remembered the grim words Ma had said, "Son, please don't do any more killing. Folks speak of you as a gunman already, and if you kill again without absolute proof of necessity, you will hang!"

Jake darted to the right, thankful for the cover of approaching darkness. But making progress in either direction was almost impossible. Brush and vines and uprooted tree trunks from the clearing at the distillery had been snaked by mule teams down toward the slough. He had the feeling his stamping, hurried flight made enough racket to rouse the dead. Rupe kept firing blindly with that shotgun, and Jake heard the smack of lead into stumps about him. Rupe's shots were getting close . . . They were spreading out. Jake heard them tramping through the brush, breathing heavily and cursing. Easing down against a large pine tree, he drew his pistol and waited. Lying silent that way, he heard them move past. Just beyond him they stopped, and he heard them whispering.

"He's somewhere close," the rough man hissed. "He's somewhere right in spittin' distance. He ain't going to try to walk out of here at night. He never could follow the road."

"His horse might. Maybe we better go back and shoot his horse."

"Hell," one man said. "You think he'd circle and go back past the light of them damn fires?"

Jake remained tensely still, thinking of the man's comments and wondering if reaching his horse really would be impossible. They moved again. Jake gauged the direction of their footsteps. It was getting darker by the minute. A dank-bodied darkness traipsed through the trees like something a man might reach out and touch. All around Jake, the tramping of footsteps continued.

"Hey!" Brack Mulvane screamed. "Me and Rupe are coming down! By God, we've got to flush him out of there!"

Jake heard the footsteps scatter, then bunch again, steadily getting closer. Except for his experience on the scout toward Mexico, he knew he might have risen and bolted. That training, and the knowledge of the vines and upthrust roots held him still. It would be better to be discovered here, while he was set to do battle, than to try to run and trip and fall in the darkness and be swarmed and overwhelmed.

But suddenly, he knew he was going to have to go into action of some kind. Someone was coming down from the distillery with lanterns. That would be Rupe and Mulvane, he guessed.

The penetrating beams of the lanterns were like the winging of two giant fireflies trying to search him out.

"There!" the man's voice said. "Get him!"

Jake rose and spun. His left fist smashed out, slamming against the bearded man's face. The man was almost against him, plain to see in the lantern beams. It was savage and merciless the way Jake took him. His shoulder drove into the man's body, toppling him back, and the heavy butt of his pistol slashed down and up and down against his bloody skull.

Other men yelled and converged upon Jake, but he hurled himself headlong and started crawling, his knees digging and his fingers clawing. He tried to move quietly, like a fox. He felt the sharp dead root of an upthrust tear flesh from his left leg, but he kept going out of the lantern light. He moved away from the maze of the forest this time and back toward his horse. He skirted the edge of the clearing around the distillery. Not a man was in sight. Everyone was looking for him. He rushed, passing the halted hack, and swiftly reached the bay. He holstered his pistol and untied the reins and mounted. The glow from the fires showed him the direction of the road along which he had previously been forced to travel. He wheeled the bay and struck out. Behind him he still heard shooting and yelling, and he knew the crew, along with Mulvane and Rupe, were searching for him in the brushy entanglements along the slough.

He must have been a mile away before he became conscious of a flowing, sticky substance in his left boot and knew the wound from the lancelike tree root had to be attended to. He had been taught the value of first aid while serving in the Confederate cavalry. He didn't figure it was a time to ignore it now. He reined slightly off the road, pulled the boot off and shielded the flame of a match to look at the wound. It looked like a pretty deep gash, but the blood was caking. He decided not to do anything about it until he found his way out of the woodlands. He knew about all he could do was trust to the instinct of the bay.

A little while later, he heard the sound of cattle bellowing. He followed the sound and came right into the middle of a large herd of cattle. He rode through them and noticed that some of the cattle carried the brand from the Spaniard range. So this was where Mulvane kept his stolen cattle! He knew he had no time to waste here now, so he led his bay back to the road.

The hours dragged past slowly while the pine forest was still clothed in pitch-black dark. At last, however, he emerged from the forest proper. A cloud cover had thinned, and he could see the glimmer of stars. This made traveling easier. Within another hour he looked ahead and saw the glimmer of lights. He wondered if the lights were coming from the tavern and hotel.

He rode closer, struck the main road, and knew his conjecture had been right. He halted the bay and looked over a long line of tied horses and a parked buggy or two. He didn't see any sign of Brack Mulvane's hack, so evidently the unscrupulous old man and Rupe hadn't beat him out of the woods. He decided to stop, go inside the hotel and see if he could do something about the wound in his leg. The muscles were getting stiff and sore and the pain was intensifying. He reached the hotel hitching rail, dismounted and tied the bay and walked inside.

A few loungers were in the lobby. He walked past them without limping, his face set straight ahead. A thin-featured night clerk met him at the counter and twirled a ledger for registering. Jake shook his head.

"I can't spend the night, pardner, but if you have bandages and some linament, I'll pay you well. I was riding through the brush country and cut my leg. I'd like to bandage the wound in a back room, if you don't mind."

"Sure," the clerk said. "Just so you pay."

Jake worked over his wound in a back room, occasionally looking out at the lights of the tavern. He thought about how strings of rotten joints like this one, probably reaching a thousand miles south and west at out-of-the-way places in the Territory, were utilizing and profiting from the whiskey made by Mulvane's crew. And such wholesale violations were spawned and allowed to flourish through corruption of local officials. Brack Mulvane had used his maneuvering in that. But there were places that Mulvane's operations didn't reach, Jake thought. Mulvane might corrupt the departments of sheriffs or local constables, deputies and city marshals, but his conniving brain couldn't wangle cooperation from the revenue men. Jake had heard his Pa speak of the far-reaching arms of Federals . . . the U.S. marshals that would not tamper with bribery.

He thought, "I fled from the officers. Now I'm going to have to get to a telegraph and send word to Fort Smith for officers to come here and break up Mulvane's gang."

He finished bandaging his wound and straightened up. He walked out, paid the clerk at the counter, then decided he would have time to go to the tavern for a short drink and a chat with Norma before Brack Mulvane or members of his crew got out of the big pine country.

He opened the door of the tavern and went inside the place, gamely hiding the fact that he was hurt. He wouldn't even let Norma know it, he thought, not at first. She was bound to learn about it, though, if he took her home that night. He ordered a drink from one of the bartenders, and looked all about the place, but didn't see Norma anywhere. He puzzled about it a moment, wondering if this could be her night off. Why hadn't he discussed more things with her? Why had he allowed the wild thrill of her presence in the forest to dull his capacity for thinking? He should have told her never to come to this place at all.

His disappointment was mounting when the grind of wheels against gravels outside caught his attention. He glanced out through a window where the lantern glowed and saw Brack Mulvane and Rupe in the hack. Rupe was still holding his shotgun. Both men were looking around the tavern entrance, evidently searching for Jake's horse. Jake was glad he had left the horse tied in front of the hotel. That portion of the area was not visible from the place where the hack had stopped. But they would be searching there, and he knew it. He drew his pistol and shoved its muzzle almost against the bartender's face.

"I know you have a hidden back entrance . . . a passageway I can use. Lead me through it! Quick! I mean business, mister! No damn foolishness here!"

The bartender's eyes bulged and his face went pasty, but he did not hesitate to obey. The noisy crowd paid little attention as Jake forced the barkeep to lead him outside the rear of the dive.

"Hell, if it's Brack Mulvane you're scared of, you ain't gonna dodge him very long anyhow," the bartender said as they paused on the chat outside. Evidently, his nerve was coming back.

"Who said I was scared of Mulvane? I'll buck him, anytime we're on equal ground."

"You'll never be on equal ground with Brack Mulvane. And you can't buck him and his crew. They have the law in these parts sewed up. Mulvane's got the city law and the sheriff right in the palm of his hand."

"Not revenue officers, though," Jake said.

The bartender's face in the dimness suddenly looked pale and ghostlike. "Take my advice, buddy. You bring the Feds down into this country and you'll be fair game for a bullet or a knife."

"Looks like I'm fair game anyhow," Jake said.

"Aw, Mulvane didn't mean to kill you out there in the woods. Not according to reports I got from Turk Munson. Turk said Mulvane and Rupe just wanted to scare the living daylights out of you."

"I didn't see Turk Munson in your dive in there. Where is he now?"

The barkeep laughed. "Turk got ants in his pants as usual. He didn't tarry here tonight. Left early with that little Clifton girl."

CHAPTER FOURTEEN

Jake stood tight-faced and silent, letting the shock surge through him and dwindle away.

The bartender's laugh faded out, and when he spoke again there was the sharpness of resentment and jealousy in his voice. "Turk was supposed to take my place behind that bar, but he's always got something else on his mind, damn him! Always shirking his job, turning the hard part over to someone else. If he'd stayed here tonight I wouldn't be lookin' down a pistol barrel, my nerves shook, not knowin' what's gonna . . . "

"Where did Turk take off to?"

"Hell, I don't know! To some filthy hotel room or maybe to a pallet out in the brush. Norma Clifton moved like her skirt was flamin', eager to get out of there. I heard that Turk took her out last night too, but was that enough for him? Hell no! He had to start makin' up to her again tonight, and took her away an hour before her shift

139

ended here. I tried to make that little hussy once, but she dodged me. She sure wasn't tryin' to dodge Turk Munson though. Not as far as I could tell."

Jake Spaniard didn't want to hear any more. There was sincere resentment in the bartender, too real to doubt. He wasn't lying. Norma had evidently gone out with Turk. The bartender wouldn't have any knowledge or reason to lie about that to Jake Spaniard.

Jake gestured with his pistol. "Start walking, mister! All the way past the rear of that hotel and out into the brush. I don't want you back inside that tavern to tell anyone anything . . . not until I'm long gone. I'll mount up and follow you for a pretty good distance. If you try anything fishy, I'll gut-shoot you and leave you for the wolves!" The bartender wheeled abruptly and started walking. Jake raced around a corner of the hotel, mounted and reined out onto the road. Off to his right, he could see the bartender walking with long strides. Jake let the bay side the man for almost a quarter of a mile through the darkness. Then Jake left him, sending the bay into a lope.

A round, orange moon floated far and forlornly through the rising mist. Gray tendrils of the mist edged the roadway, and even above the pound of the bay's hoofbeats, he could hear the pulsing of life on the range . . . He thought of the night before, and the sight of Turk Munson's hack, and the sound of Norma Clifton screaming. But those screams hadn't amounted to anything.

140

A girl acted different ways with different men, but it all summed up the same. No telling how many times Norma had been with Turk and with other men. The fact that she had gone against Turk only showed that she had sensed something better in Jake Spaniard, so she had sided him on the old forest road in order to lure him to her later. It was a galling thought that left him hurt and bitter as he rode.

A man couldn't trust a woman now, not these days. Look how Trudene had done, warming up to Jake's brother while he was away in Mexico. Look at all the wild-living people, young and middle-aged and even sometimes the old. Look at a beautiful woman like Sabina Mulvane, crazed for men. Jake's mind did a slow double take. He smiled bitterly in the darkness. Hadn't it been that way with him too, with the pretty *señoritas* at the fiestas in Mexico? Women flaunt their appeal, and men take the bait, and that's the way it goes. He knew he didn't have any right to condemn either Norma or Trudene for giving in to urgings that had trapped HIM, many a-time . . . But he had loved Norma so and had trusted her and thought she belonged to him. He had fought his desire for Sabina Mulvane and it was partly because of his love and loyalty for Norma. What was a man to do when he wanted to be honest, to change his ways, and the girl he loved was wild and bent on deceiving him?

His thoughts cut off, and the urgency at hand returned as he heard the swift thunder of hoofbeats behind him. Mulvane was getting the word out to his henchmen. Jake reined off the road and stopped the bay and waited. He realized the night was swarming with armed riders, all of them searching for him. He knew it would be foolish to stay on the road while riders were desperately searching. He kept the bay to a slow walk at the edge of the timber, ready at an instant's warning to ride into the brush. Mulvane would certainly have men on the road near Hanson. Other riders would be stationed to watch the old Spaniard home.

It was an aggravating dilemma. Jake knew he had to somehow slip into Sallisaw and get word out by telegraph to U.S. deputy marshals. Somehow, he had to get to that telegraph office ... but how? The angle of another road came into view, connecting with the main route beside which he was riding. High on the mountainside to his left, he heard a dog bark, then the shrill whinny of a horse. He checked his mount, gauging his position. He realized he was crossing the road that led up the mountain to Elmer and Clarissa Gordon's place. Even as he looked that way, he saw a lighted lamp being set near a window. It was late, but Clarissa was up, he thought. The barking of the dog continued. Jake wondered if some of Mulvane's riders were fooling around the Gordon place. The thought made him instantly turn the bay into the side road. He knew he had to find out.

He approached the house cautiously, watching intently for any moving objects in the light of the climbing moon. He kept the bay to the edge of the road, where mattings of pine needles muffled the horse's hoofbeats. In a few minutes he was near the corrals. He circled them slowly, his pistol in his hand. The barking of the dog became a constant clamor. Then, as he neared a corner of the barn, a voice abruptly challenged him.

"Don't come any closer, mister! If you do I'll shoot!"

It was the voice of Clarissa Gordon. It had been three years, but he instantly recognized it. Her voice had come from behind the heavy slats of the horse corral.

"Clarissa . . . It's me . . . Jake Spaniard."

"Jake?! . . . I can't believe it! What are you doing here this time of night?"

"It's a pretty long story, Clarissa. I don't suppose I have time to tell it all . . . Has anyone been prowling around here tonight?"

"Yes, but I heard them ride away pretty fast." She materialized from the shadows, opening the corral gate and stepping outside. He saw she was holding a long rifle. "And you *DO* have time to tell me that story! Get down, put your horse in the corral and come to the house with me." She moved closer. "Jake Spaniard! Good heavens, it's been three years or more."

"Are you certain I won't be bothering you, Clarissa?"

"Of course I'm certain! Get down off that horse, and let's go have a look at you in the light."

Within minutes they were entering the spacious front room of the huge country home. Clarissa Gordon turned to look at him in the lamplight. She offered her hand.

"Jake Spaniard! . . . You're bigger than ever. I heard rumors you were coming home, and just knew you'd visit us the minute you got back!"

"How are you, Clarissa? Is everything going well?"

It was merely an effort to put her at ease. He knew things were not well with her.

She released his hand and backed up a step. "I said 'us,' Jake, but you probably know by now. Elmer's dead. He tripped or something while he was hunting one day, and his gun went off."

Jake looked at her, thinking how much she had aged in three years. He thought, too, of Brack Mulvane's taunting, insinuating words, "Elmer Gordon isn't living anymore." Had it really been an accident, he wondered?

Then Clarissa noticed the splotches of blood on the leg of his trousers. "Jake!" She touched his arm. "You've been hurt!"

"It doesn't amount to much," he said.

She looked at him steadily. "Are you going to tell me what happened?"

He told her, as briefly as he could. "And my problem now is getting to the telegraph office in Sallisaw," he said. "I need to contact the closest U.S. deputy marshal I can find."

"Why, there's one *in* Sallisaw, Hector Grant."

"When did a deputy marshal come here?"

"Not long after you left. He and Elmer became

close friends, and Elmer kept him posted on some of the rackets . . . but Elmer knew about so few."

"What's the marshal's main duties here?"

"Protecting the Arkansas-Oklahoma Indians, I heard."

"You sure he isn't paid off by Brack Mulvane?"

Clarissa frowned and said thoughtfully, "I don't believe a man like Hector Grant could be bribed. He was discharged from the Confederate Army with great honors. He's a man who demands respect."

"Not very many hours ago, I got the idea that Thad Brill was running everything concerning law enforcement in and around Sallisaw," Jake said.

"Well, that's true, as far as any affairs that don't concern Federal law," Clarissa said. "Frankly, Hector Grant spends most of his time at the Indian villages, helping to see that the tribes get enough to eat from the agencies. But Grant would step in and help you, if you could get him word. And he could bring in all the other Federal men you need."

Jake paced the floor, favoring his aching leg. "My problem's ever getting to the marshal. Mulvane and Brill will have every road blocked, I know."

Clarissa parted the curtains of a window and looked out into the night. When she turned back to Jake her face and eyes were filled with determination.

"It will be daylight before too long, Jake. And I'll tell you what I'm going to do. I'll give you a bed in a back room so you can get some rest and as soon as it's full day, I'll go into town . . . and contact Marshal Grant myself!"

"No. I can't let you get involved in this."

"Involved? What a word, coming from you, Jake! What we all need to do is get involved and break up Brack Mulvane's vile whiskey trade! Now don't you argue with me! I'll go to town in one of our best buckboards, and if I get stopped I'll tell those that stop me I'm on my way after a load of feed. After I reach town, I'll somehow reach Hector Grant and send him out here. You can explain to him exactly what you need."

Jake watched her, and seeing the determination mounting in her eyes, knew that further argument would be futile. Clarissa Gordon was a determined woman. She had fully made up her mind. And why not let her strike a blow against the man who was probably responsible for her husband's death, Jake thought? Finally he nodded agreement. She led the way to a back room and pointed out his bed.

He knew he would not sleep, but he could lie there and listen and get up occasionally through the rest of the night to watch for prowling riders. And after Clarissa had gone, he would have a comparatively safe hiding place. He could watch the main road at the foot of the mountain, and the side road and trails. . . . He lay back against the pillows, fully clothed, listening to the soft footsteps of Clarissa in another room. Finally the house was silent. The dog had ceased barking. There were no sounds except those of cicadas and occasional whippoorwills. . . . He hadn't known how weary he was, how much punishment his body had taken. Despite his effort to stay awake, sleep finally slid over him like a shroud.

The sun was high when he roused up. He knew, without going to the corrals and barn to see, that Clarissa had long since gone to town. In fact, when he looked out through a front window, he saw her on the loaded buckboard, returning. He walked out to the barn and helped her unharness the team. She didn't say much until they were back inside the house, then she faced him and started talking swiftly, her eyes shining.

"Marshal Grant has been trying for a long time to trace down things against Brack Mulvane. His efforts have been blocked by the sheriff, the police and by Thad Brill. Now Marshal Grant is happy about a chance for a breakthrough. He will ride out within the hour to talk to you."

"Did you get stopped anywhere on the road?"

"Yes. One time. By Thad Brill and another officer, a deputy sheriff, I think. They just asked why I was driving into town so early. I told them it was to beat the heat and that I was going in after some sack feed for our horses. I made it clear it was no business of his, and drove on. After that, it was easy to reach the marshal. I just went out the back door of the feed store and circled around to the marshal's house."

"I don't know how to thank you, Clarissa. Danged if I didn't fall off to sleep."

She laughed. "That will do you good. I'll fix breakfast for you now, and you'll be ready for talk when the marshal gets here."

U.S. Deputy Marshal Hector Grant came riding up the side road toward the Gordon country home before an hour had passed. He was a big man with a friendly handshake, rugged features and keen eyes. Jake got down to business. He made it strong.

"Mulvane's whiskey operations are twice as large as most legal distilleries," he told the marshal. "And Mulvane has gathered around him some of the worst thugs I've ever seen. Mulvane and his crew are probably tied up with more angles of crime than you can untangle in months, but it's a start to know the ring leader of the bunch. I'll take you and your men to that distillery and side them until the job of pinning the goods on Mulvane is done."

Crackling questions came at him from the marshal, probing for sincerity in Jake's talk. The big marshal wanted something on his background, his authority and references.

Jake said in a clipped voice, "I've just come home after several months' travel in west Texas and Mexico. I know what special detail is, because I was raised in this land of local bribery. There are plenty of ways you can check my record, but if you're going to let red tape block your actions for days, I'm going to raise some of my old Fort Smith buddies and go in and break up that ring." Jake paused and glanced at Clarissa Gordon. "There may even be some murder charges come out of this, if the investigation goes deep enough."

"You want me to contact marshals in Fort Smith or Muskogee, then contact you? Is that right? Or would deputy marshals closer in be best?"

"The closer and the faster the better," Jake said.

"Where will we contact you?"

Jake hesitated, thinking again that some of Mulvane's men would probably be watching for him to come out of the forest near home. But he doubted that, even in daylight, any of Mulvane's hirelings would be capable of blocking a man trained on the scout. Certainly they couldn't block him from reaching Ma and Lige in the dark.

"I'll be at home, barring bad luck," he said. "Anyone in the region can tell you where. And you can minimize any danger for me if you manage to get word to that tavern and hotel that a Federal raid is shaping up. Tell the bartenders to relay the message . . ."

Marshal Hector Grant said in amazement, "You are asking us to signal our punches?"

Jake said decisively, "Most interests of the man running that distillery lie right in and around Sallisaw. I know where the still is and can prove who has been operating it. A man can't wrap up such big business in a few hours and flee the country. I'm sure he sells all over, but headquarters are here."

"You think your life may be in danger?"

"It was a few hours ago," Jake said. "It could be again."

"You're sure asking an unorthodox maneuver," the marshal said. "But I reckon we'll do it. Anything else?"

"Yeah. When will your men be here?"

"You just get home, stay put and trust us for fast action," the marshal said. He shook hands with Jake, bowed to Clarissa, went out and mounted, then left.

Jake looked at Clarissa Gordon. He realized she had been listening to every word. And she had evidently caught the drift of the situation rapidly. Her face, more thin and lined than it had been earlier, looked tense and pale.

"Jake, you said something about . . . murder. Who. . . ?"

He was aware of vast compassion for her. He took her arm and led her to a chair. She was thinking of her dead husband, he knew. He drew up another chair and sat down facing her.

"I don't know anything definite, Clarissa," he said. "But it seems strange to me that a man like Elmer, someone born and raised in the woodlands and used to handling guns all his life, would have tripped and accidentally killed himself. Did he ever have bad trouble with Brack Mulvane?"

"Not too much . . . only that he blocked Mulvane once from building a large tavern out on the road too close to our place. Elmer wouldn't stand for that. But there really wasn't any bad trouble with Mulvane himself. There was worse trouble between Elmer and Turk Munson. You remember how Turk used to try to court me all through summer subscription school? Well, he made some advances after Elmer and I were married. Elmer never got over that, never forgot it. He cornered Turk, and they fought . . . Oh, I wish I had never told Elmer about the things Turk said to me!"

Jake rose and stood looking at her. He knew that he had been wrong in more ways than one. Elmer Gordon had been dead for several months, but Clarissa had loved him and was still grieving for him. He had been wrong thinking that no woman or girl could be trusted. There were still honest ones like Clarissa in this world. All girls weren't like Norma Clifton, beautiful and deceptive, tricking a man without qualms, playing one man against another.

Clarissa Gordon must have sensed the restlessness and desperation that suddenly burdened him. She rose. "Jake, what started this trouble between you and Brack Mulvane?"

"Mulvane wants my big pine country and all the grazing land and cattle. He wants the pines left for a hiding place for his whiskey-making operations. He's trying to block every effort I make to raise money to develop my land."

"Did you try to borrow money from him?"

"No. I tried one bank, though, and I found out where I stand. I'm a hill country rancher that no banker will loan money to. The owners of banks,

151

or loan companies, think I don't have enough sense to promote anything profitable."

Clarissa's glance brightened. "I have money, Jake. I trust you, and know Elmer would have too."

"Thanks," he said. He thought it over a moment, but there was despondency in him because of Norma's fickle ways. "I don't know right now. Sometime I may come talk to you. Thanks anyhow."

He moved to the door, and his despondency intensified. The substance of the dream wasn't so great any more. He had woven many of those dreams around the thought of some loyal girl siding him.

He thanked Clarissa again and left her. As he mounted and rode, he was wondering if those messages about the impending raid were already being relayed to Mulvane and his men.

In a case like this, it was hard to judge whether a man had done the right thing or the wrong thing, Jake thought. He remembered Marshal Grant's reluctance to signal the impending raid. Maybe it would have been better to have taken Mulvane wholly by surprise. But he knew as he rode that he didn't want it that way, and it was largely because of an ingrained reluctance in him to take advantage of anyone. And he knew why it was. Deep in his mind was the bitter memory of a cordon of revenue men, converging upon poor old Pa, one time years ago.... But Jake figured that in at least one way, he had been thinking solid. Mulvane's men would probably be pulled off the chase after him, because Brack Mulvane wasn't dumb enough to commit murder, or have any of his men do it, when he knew Federal officers were aware of what was going on.

And it was as he had told the marshal: It would be impossible for Mulvane and his crew to destroy evidence of whiskey-making operations within a few hours. About all Mulvane and his gang could hope to do was come out of the deep woods and give up. Mulvane wouldn't abandon his vast holdings in and around Sallisaw. He would plan on legal maneuvering to get him free. It wasn't until next day, when Jake was home with Ma and Lige, that he discovered how badly he had misplayed his hand.

CHAPTER FIFTEEN

Leaving Clarissa's place, Jake had traveled cautiously through the forest, stopping often, listening and concealing himself throughout that day. He had ridden home under cover of darkness, his pistol at the ready in his hand.

The moon was high, almost as bright as day over the woodlands. There had been no horses in sight nor men on foot about the place when he pulled up by the barnyard at home. A lamp was lighted in the front room of the house. He had found Ma and Lige up, waiting and worrying about him. Jake told them the story while he cleaned up, dressed the cut on his leg and ate a meal that Ma warmed up from him. Lige showed embarrassment around him at first, and he knew it was because of Trudene Clifton. But later, as his story advanced, the embarrassment faded and Lige's face became tense with concern.

"I figured somethin' was goin' on there, after a bunch of jaspers collared me once," Lige said.

His head lowered. "They beat me up. Ought to of done somethin' about it, but Mulvane had a lease. I . . . "

"It's all right, Lige. Federal officers will be here soon, I figure along about sundown at the latest. We'll jerk a kink in Brack Mulvane's tail that he won't be able to untangle for quite a spell."

They sat and talked about it through the night, Ma and Jake and Lige, and out in the front yard the old Padge hound bawled down the moon and howled in the daybreak.

Ma was just blowing out the flickering kerosene lamp when Jake heard the sound of hoofbeats approaching from the direction of the Clifton place. Jake rose and went to a window. He saw two riders coming around the turn over a hummock, and instantly recognized them. They were Turk Munson and the Pawnee lawman, Thad Brill. He turned and faced his brother, who had stepped up beside him. "Lige, get Pa's old double-barreled shotgun. Load both muzzles, go out the back and come around and give me cover if I need it."

Lige hesitated, licking dry lips. The old fear was in him, and Jake knew it. For the first time he was harshly impatient with it.

"Don't stand here with your bare face hanging out! Get that gun and do like I told you! Hear?"

Lige stood like someone struck dumb, staring from Jake to Ma.

"You heard your brother, Lige," Ma said. "There may be trouble for Jake. You're a

155

Spaniard, you hear me? You do as your brother says!"

Lige turned with dragging footsteps and reached to the hickory racks above the kitchen door. He took down the double-barreled shotgun just as the two riders halted near the front yard gate.

Jake went to the front door, opened it and stepped out onto the porch. There was no pretense that this was a friendly visit. Jake drew his pistol and had it in his hand when he stopped. Turk got off his horse with a galling brazenness, his big shoulders swaying and a half-smoked cigarette dangling from his lips. But Brill . . . for the first time, Thad Brill revealed reluctance and uncertainty. He dismounted too, but he stood by his horse and waited. It amazed Jake, but Thad Brill didn't even have a gun on his hip.

Turk came walking toward the gate, and Jake stepped down from the porch and went to meet him. They stopped, facing each other. Turk said, "I rode over to tell you something, Spaniard."

"Get it said!"

One of Turk's hands lifted, touching the side of his face that Jake's fists had beaten black and blue. But none of the swaggering brazenness went out of Turk. There was too much hatred for Jake in him. Evidence of it spilled plainly from his heated gaze.

"You'll have to get willing to negotiate, Spaniard," Turk said.

Jake's coppery eyes raked him, revealing

hatred that matched anything in Turk. It had always been that way, and it was worse in him now as he thought of Turk's relations with Norma Clifton.

"I don't negotiate anything with you, Munson," Jake said.

Thad Brill's voice, lacking in its usual drawling confidence, said from beside his horse. "Spaniard, you ought to listen to what Turk has to say. It's one reason I rode along . . . to try to get you to listen. You're goin' to have to call off that Federal raid."

"You getting in hot water, Brill? You in too deep with Mulvane?"

Brill swallowed. He gestured at Turk. "Maybe we both are, but that's beside the point. I've been euchered into doin' some things that maybe I oughtn't to have done for Mulvane, but the main thing now is that . . . "

"Shut up, Thad!" Turk ordered. "Hell, I've got the nerve to tell him! Spaniard, if you don't call off that raid, it's likely you and your bud, Lige, won't be seein' them Clifton girls again."

Turk Munson's very presence was enough to spur Jake to violence, let alone the mocking way he spoke. Jake leaped at him, grabbed a handful of Turk's shirt collar and twisted it.

"What are you trying to say to me, you rutting-minded son-of-a-bitch?"

Turk's hands went up to Jake's wrist and he started to fight free. Then his glance cut over Jake's shoulder and riveted. Lige came around the corner of the house and levelled the double-

157

barreled shotgun at Turk's head.

"Spill it all out, Turk!" Jake grated. "Tell me everything you know!"

Turk's eyes had bulged at the first sight of Lige, and now as Jake released him, he touched his throat and coughed. It was plain that sudden terror was gnawing at his alcohol-damaged heart.

"Mulvane and Rupe, and that rough-bearded man, they've got Norma and Trudene Clifton," he finally choked.

"Where?"

"They're all out at the still. Mulvane says if you don't call off the Feds and give him a chance to hide evidence, he's goin' to shoot both girls and dump 'em in that old cattle dippin' vat near the creek."

"Hell!" Jake said disbelievingly. "Mulvane wouldn't lay himself wide open for hanging that way."

Turk squirmed as Lige stepped up and pushed the muzzles of the shotgun into his belly. Lige's voice, slow but filled with power that amazed Jake, quietly demanded. "You tell us again what may happen to Trudene. How did Brack Mulvane get hold of her?"

Turk choked. "I don't know exactly who got Trudene. It was the bearded man, I think. . . . Mulvane tricked me into taking Norma to him. Told me to tell her if she would come and talk to him, he would give her a good job in one of his better places. That might have made her happy,

158

the family being so poor and all, and her Pa sick all the time on whiskey. Mulvane said for me to take her to his office in town, but him and Rupe jumped us from the brush and took her into the backwoods. Rupe told me then they already had Trudene, and hinted that Mulvane was turning into a wild man. I don't think Mulvane heard Rupe say that, but Mulvane ordered me to come here and warn you to call off that raid on his still."

Much of Turk Munson's talk was a deep droning in Jake's ears, because in his mind was the thought of Norma, happily leaving the tavern with Turk because she thought she was going to get a better job in a nicer place. She hadn't gone with Turk because she wanted to be with him, but because she had been thinking of her family, of what a better job could do for her folks. An avalanche of self-condemnation piled up on Jake because he had misjudged her. Turk Munson wasn't lying, because he was looking at Lige Spaniard, the man he had often called "that crazy loon." There was terror in Turk Munson, because he could see Lige's fingers curling around the trigger of that cocked shotgun.

Turk's eyes suddenly did a wild swiveling, as if panic were strangling him. "You Spaniards sure better listen! I know what my old stepdaddy will do. I know what he *CAN* do too! He not only told me right flat out that he would kill them girls, but that if I didn't come here and tell you, some dark night I'd get it in the back with a pistol slug or a knife, or some way that might look like an accident . . . "

"Like Elmer Gordon was killed?"

Turk looked at Jake and appeared to find breathing difficult. Then he said in a rush, "The reason Brack Mulvane has got by is because some of the better folks have underestimated him, all that power he has! They don't think he can kill either. He don't look like a killer, but I know he is. And half the businesses he fronts for around here are fakes. His money all comes from whiskey trade . . . cold cash that he keeps buried in the hills . . . And I know he can kill them girls and leave by boat down Skin Bayou. In the real heart of the country, he might never be trapped until he got ready to go down to the Coast, then maybe over to Cuba somewhere."

"That's right, Spaniard," Thad Brill said. "It's the truth."

Lige backed up with the shotgun. Glancing at his brother, Jake was surprised at the determined strength that showed in Lige's face. Lige was thinking of Trudene Clifton, and the old fears were dwindling in him, blotted out by his love for her.

Lige would go into the back country to try to protect her. Jake sensed that urge in his brother now. Ma did, too, because abruptly she was there beside Lige, clutching his strong arms.

"Don't you do anything rash, now, son."

"I won't, Ma. But I know that country. I know the place to go. I got pounded there once and didn't say anything about it. I didn't go back in there because I was scared of Brack Mulvane's

160

crew. But I ain't scared no more, and I know where to find Trudene and Norma too."

There was a moment of silence. The sun rose through the treetops that ringed the clearing, dripping golden mist and fog. Brill's voice finally drifted across the silence. "It won't do any good for you boys to go into the woods armed. Mulvane specified that."

Jake wheeled upon him and shoved him away from the horse. Inside Brill's saddlebags were two fully loaded pistols. Jake thrust one inside his belt and handed the other to Lige.

"Give Ma the double-barrel," he told Lige. "Ma, you sit down on the steps of the porch and keep that gun trained on Turk and Brill. Keep it cocked and ready. It won't miss. Hold both of them here until the Federals come. I'm not waiting. Let's go Lige. We'll strike through the woods on foot."

They moved in unison, straight across the open rangeland and into the heart of the forest. The old Padge hound followed them. The pads of the dog made almost no sound, but Jake asked, "Lige, do you reckon the hound will bark and give us away?"

Lige glanced at the hound with deep affection and shook his head. "He'll help us if we get off the trail. Once we strike a trail, and ol' Padge smells that bunch, nothing can shake him off."

Steadily, making as little sound as possible, the brothers forged ahead. They passed the place where only two days ago Jake had known that brief time with Norma. He was burdened briefly by a renewal of self-condemnation; then he shrugged it off. How could a man think any other way than the way he had thought after knowing deception in so many and after hearing the barkeep's talk? But Jake Spaniard vowed as he strode along that he would never distrust Norma Clifton again. A faint chill touched his body. Dread and fear mounted in him that he might not find her alive. If those Federal officers failed to wait, as he had directed, Mulvane might do away with Trudene and Norma, grab his fortune in cash and disappear.

Heat coiled up from the floor of the forest as the sun rose higher. The croaking of frogs and bullish voices of wild yearlings faded away. The only things stirring were birds overhead and a few cottonmouth snakes that slithered out to sun themselves on the banks of the many sloughs. Jake's admiration for Lige grew with the passing minutes. Lige was apparently tireless, traveling with the ease of a big buck deer, light-footed in spite of his heavy body. He had somehow mastered whatever had happened to his mind after that old whiskey war beating. They moved on, slowing occasionally and listening, while the old Padge hound crept beside them, lifting his pads high and setting them down softly. His muzzle moved right and left as he sniffed the breeze. Then Jake smelled the first stink of soured whiskey mash, and at the same instant heard a sound. It was a hollow boom and swish, close at hand, and instantly he knew what it was. Someone was prying over those copper boilers, dumping their pottail leavings from yesterday's run, trying to destroy evidence of Mulvane's work.

Jake signaled to Lige and took the lead, moving cautiously through the vines and creepers. When he came out to where he could see the distillery, he realized they were just across the slough from it, but the thing that was going on there was plainly visible. Three men were working hard and as silently as possible, dumping barrels of mash that were lined along the edge of the clearing, and overturning the barrels and the copper drums and rolling them into the depths of the slough. The third man of the group Jake recognized as the bearded, gnarly-handed old swamp native who had operated the ferry on Jake's first trip in. The oldster worked without obvious perturbation, but the others sweated and cursed in low voices. Finally one of them stopped, ran his mash-soaked hands down the sides of his hips and straightened up.

"Hell," he said in a harsh voice. "We'll never get this job done. It'd take a month. How the hell we gonna wipe out signs of a hundred-barrel outfit in one day?"

The old man kept working and didn't seem to hear, but the other man stopped and looked at his companion who had voiced the protest.

"I think we're fools," the second man said. "Chances is, if we stay here, we'll be the only ones caught."

"I say to hell with this job!" the first spokesman declared. "Mulvane and Rupe and ol' sad-sack Whistling Britches and the others, they've got away to their hidin' place, and think of the two lovelies they've got with them!"

"Yeah," the other agreed. "And what've we got here 'cept stinkin' cooc and not even no decent pottail liquor to drink? I say we sneak out to the road and go get somethin' fit to eat and drink at that tavern!"

Lige pressed forward, starting to move past Jake, but Jake barred him with an outstretched arm. "Let them move on, Lige," he whispered. "We won't have anyone here to contend with except the old man. Besides, they're all just hired help."

Lige nodded in agreement, but impatience to be at someone's throat was plainly riding him.

Abruptly, the two men with the oldster waved at him contemptuously and headed into the woods. The old man watched them vanish, then calmly went back to work.

Jake and Lige eased around the edge of the slough and slipped up behind the old man. But he was sharp for his age and quick like an animal. He sensed their presence and wheeled around, and it was almost like magic, the way his slimy right hand snaked a pistol from beneath the bib of his beer-soaked overalls. He was levelling the gun when Jake collared him.

Jake knew an instant of near desperation, not because of his fear of a bullet, but because he didn't want that gun to go off. He squeezed the old man's bony wrist in steely fingers, tilting the arm up and trying to shake the pistol loose. Lige was behind the old duffer, trying to grab the gun too. But the old man's strength was amazing. Jake felt the tendons of the old fellow's wrist straining as his finger crooked on the trigger of the gun.

It exploded, then dropped from the old man's hand while echoes of the shot tumbled against the tree trunks in resounding smacks. Jake released the old man and backed up, listening to the echoes and knowing that Mulvane must surely be warned. Anything could happen now, including the deaths of Trudene and Norma Clifton.

CHAPTER SIXTEEN

It took iron control for Jake to hold himself in leash, to keep his tightly gripped hands from opening and going at the old man's throat. He managed it, and said with all the calmness he could muster. "The jig's up for you, mister. Federal officers will be here in a little while. You might as well talk up, tell us where Brack Mulvane is."

The old country native merely blinked, his bloodshot eyes showing no fear, no emotion of any kind. He was one in a million, Jake knew, the kind a man seldom met. The knowledge spawned a faint admiration in Jake Spaniard. Jake felt that this old-timer could well be Absalom Spaniard, bearded and dirtier and older, but the same kind of man in many ways, born with a galvanized iron lining in his stomach that could withstand the ravages of whiskey taken daily for half a century and not much harm done at all. Maybe this old man's contemporaries had died very young, trying to match him but eventually writhing in agony in the swamp muck, fighting unimaginable demons and hordes of snakes with a thousand heads. So the old man stood alone, and about the only difference between him and Absalom Spaniard was that Jake's father had been blessed with a bit more pride that had fired him to try to accumulate things, including the acres and acres of the territory where this bearded old duffer lived.

Then a thought stilled Jake Spaniard. Where DID the old duffer live?

"Where's your house, mister?"

The old man looked at Lige, then back to Jake. A foxy humor flashed out of his fearless glance. Jake knew then that the old man wouldn't talk. You could kick his shins or scorch his feet . . . cuff him, castrate him or kill him . . . and he wouldn't tell the whereabouts of the man who had hired him to work at this illicit whiskey trade. Working at the trade was as much a part of the old man's existence as breathing, and the man who hired him was his god.

"Fine a rope somewhere, Lige," Jake said. "Rope, cord or anything. Tie him up."

Lige searched among the stacks of burlap and finally came up with some strong cord. He wrestled the old man to the earth and bound him. Then Jake and Lige headed again into the brush.

This time Lige was in the lead, and Jake sensed a growing assurance in him. Finally Lige stopped and looked around.

"That time they beat me up . . . it was about here, and after I'd staggered around a long time, I saw an old hewn-post shanty. Looked like it had been there for fifty years. But it was lived in. I remember seeing smoke from a chimney. I kind of thought it might be where one of Pa's old moonshining buddies was squatting on our land, and I just let it be. But Mulvane and his bunch could be hidin' there now."

Jake nodded. They moved on.

A clatter of hoofbeats sounded far down the slope of the forest as a group of fast-moving but unseen riders passed. Jake's eyes narrowed as he touched Lige's shoulder and they stood a moment listening. He wondered if the riders were U.S. deputy marshals, already storming through the woods. Annoyance stirred in him. That gunshot had been enough to warn Brack Mulvane and his crew, if they were anywhere close. Now if riders kept coming, Mulvane might panic and do anything. If he knew Federal officers were approaching, he would turn into a desperate man. Jake knew a moment of dark despondency. He sure had bungled this job. . . .

He and Lige passed through a jumble of boulders and then, at the same instant, they heard a strange sound. They paused a moment and listened. In the vastness of the forest it was a puzzling sound, almost unbelievable. The old Padge hound stopped, one paw lifted and his hackles rising and a tremulous whine starting in his throat.

"Padge, you hush it!" Lige whispered. He

looked oddly at Jake, and Jake looked at him.

Somewhere below that jumble of boulders, yonder ahead in the woodland, a girl was singing. It was an unmistakable, vibrant, exuberant sound: a girl's voice lifted in a lilting old mountain song. Jake Spaniard went toward the sound like someone drawn by a magnet. He had heard Norma Clifton sing when she was a small girl, and he recognized her voice. His mind centered upon the sound of it. In his heart was the warm sense that she was alive and feeling well.

Recent training in cavalry maneuvering made Jake move with instinctive quietness, but Lige, pressing upon his heels, was eager and making too much racket now. Awareness of that made Jake slow.

When Lige came up beside him, they parted some vines and intently searched the woodlands. Directly ahead was the old, log shack that Lige had mentioned. In front of it were two curtained hacks and a group of saddled horses. Jake saw Brack Mulvane, pacing restlessly to and fro beside one of the hacks. He was bareheaded, and for once, his white shirt looked wrinkled and stained and his black string tie was askew. Beside Mulvane, leaning against the side of the hack and looking toward the shanty, was Rupe. Apparently, he was never without that sawed-off shotgun. Rupe had the gun in his hand now.

However, Mulvane and Rupe held Jake's glance only for an instant. He looked toward the shanty, and his amazement grew by leaps and bounds at what he saw. Norma Clifton, wearing the same red skirt she had worn that first night in the tavern, was singing the mountain song and dancing, her bare feet and legs flashing in the sun. In a dark circle beyond her, watching her avidly, were five men. Norma's dancing partner, now laughing and circling her widely, was the old bearded man.

"Look!" Lige whispered. "There's Trudene . . . sitting yonder on that log."

Jake looked, and it was a moment filled with both tension and revelation. The revelation was wrapped up in the plain contrast between Trudene and Norma. Trudene was sitting dejectedly on the rotting log, her face down in her hands one moment, then lifting in obvious fright and worry; she was a picture of despair while her young sister danced. Trudene had always been that way, quick to worry and fret, but not Norma. No doubt Norma was frightened too, but she wasn't letting anyone know it. She was trapped and probably fully aware of it, but in the eyes of the watching men, she was having herself a ball.

Resentment stirred in Jake because she was dancing with the man, but he fought the feeling and conquered it. He had made a vow about Norma Clifton. He loved her and wanted her, no matter how she acted or what she did. He watched her hands sweep back her hair in the old way. He saw her feet going swiftly this way and that, and he knew he wanted her, needed her aliveness siding him all through the years. A man didn't question too much when he needed a certain girl.

Then, as Lige started toward the scene and Jake reached out to block him, revelation came in a different way. Rupe suddenly left the hack and in a long stride went toward Norma and the man.

Jake heard the sharp, commanding sound of Rupe's voice. "Stop it! Boss-man said cut it off!"

The bearded man stopped and lifted his face to stare at Rupe, but Norma kept singing and dancing, snapping her fingers sideward at Rupe in a teasing way.

"Cut that out, you little hussy!" Brack Mulvane yelled. He moved up behind Rupe, his face contorted with fury. "You're doing that deliberately to inflame my men!"

Norma kept dancing, looking around at the gang and laughing and snapping her fingers at them. "Why, Mister Mulvane," she said, "are you too old to get inflamed?"

"I'll make you think old, damn you!" Mulvane snarled. He had lost all his accustomed reserve. "Rupe, slap the damned little bitch's face!"

Rupe started toward Norma, but the man dancing with Norma, abruptly blocked his way.

"Get back over there and mind your own business!" he growled. "Me and this chick here, we're havin' ourselves some fun!"

He had his mind on one thing, a certain thing he enjoyed more than anything else in the world, and he wasn't going to let Rupe stop it. His left hand lifted, sweeping Rupe's gun aside. But Rupe was a killer, and when he went into deadly action, he did it fast. He jerked the gun around and thrust the muzzle straight against the man's left side. He squeezed the trigger, and the explosion crashed and echoed. Blood spurted. The man tottered sideward, groveling in the throes of death.

"Now, Lige!" Jake ordered. "Now's the time!"

They lunged through the brush without caution, because now there was no need for it. The gang near the cabin stood frozen. Norma had stopped her dancing and was rushing toward Trudene. Rupe heard Lige and Jake coming. Desperately, he broke the sawed-off and was hurriedly reloading it. He spun, the gun stabbing toward Jake, but Jake's pistol roared as he killed Rupe with two shots through the brain.

"Keep that gang covered, Lige! Have Norma take their guns."

Jake wheeled around then, his eyes questing for Brack Mulvane.

But Mulvane had turned and fled and was already in one of the halted hacks. Jake caught a glimpse of Mulvane as the latter leaned out, threshing at the rumps of the team with a whip. The team lurched ahead and turned, the wheels of the hack skidding. Mulvane pushed a short pistol between the curtains of the hack and took one fast shot at Jake as Jake leaped and grabbed at one of the bridles of the team. His handhold caught, but the speed of the team jerked it free. The hack was like a black-clothed demon, lurching away wildly between the trees.

Jake fired, but doubted if his bullets scored a hit. And the black hack disappeared. But he heard sounds echoing through the forest and knew it was short reprieve for Brack Mulvane. At first, there were shouted commands to halt from approaching U.S. deputy marshals, then the resounding boom of many pistol shots. After that there was a brief silence, then the pounding of hoofbeats as the marshals rode on up the slope.

Jake turned and moved up beside Norma and Trudene. When Norma turned to face him, he saw the strain in her eyes and the paleness of her features.

"Thank heavens, Jake," she said softly, and there was the same relief and gratefulness in her voice that he had heard when he had jerked Turk off her on the old forest road.

Jake looked at the group of men in front of the cabin.

"Stretch out flat on the porch there until the marshals get here," he commanded.

They obeyed, but one of them lifted his head to stare at Jake and snickered. "I've got a feeling about them gunshots I heard," he said. "Mulvane met them Federals . . . That widow of his, man, can she have fun now with Mulvane's money, no strings attached . . . And you, Spaniard . . . you could sample that to your heart's content, now Mulvane's probably dead!"

Jake merely looked at him, hating him for saying it in Norma's presence. Then the clatter of hoofbeats was right at hand as the marshals entered the clearing. There were six of them, led by Marshal Hector Grant.

"Mulvane tried a wild getaway and we had to

kill him," Grant said without visible emotion. He dismounted, shook hands with Jake and Lige and introduced the other marshals. He recognized Marshal Heck Thomas, who handed Jake a telegram.

Jake read the telegram and found that "due to evidence during investigations in Fort Smith," he was cleared of all charges there and nothing in light of the law hung over his head due to discovery of cattle ring in eastern Indian Territory and his discovery of whiskey trade.

"We'll wrap everything up later, including the ones your Ma was holding at home. We'll also want to come back and have a look at the whiskey operations today," Grant said. There was a pause and then the marshal said, "There'll be a fast-drop hanging at Old Whiskey Smith next month. You want to witness it?" Spaniard shook his head and said, "No."

Grant paused and looked at Trudene and Norma, then at Jake and Lige. He gestured to the nearby hack. "You people want to ride?"

"No," Jake said. "Thanks, but we'll walk out. It isn't far, not as a crow would fly."

Grant smiled and looked up toward the tops of the tall pines. "Be hard to see even a crow flying, through such fine timber as this."

"Yep." Jake looked up too, and he was thinking of Clarissa Gordon and her offer to lend him money to develop the land. "I'm going to be pretty busy getting this timber out to market before too long."

"That's good. Thanks for putting us onto

Mulvane's whiskey deals here, Spaniard."

"You're welcome. And thanks for coming in time."

Jake watched the marshals round up the five on the porch and ride away, and suddenly he remembered the old man tied at the still. This cabin was no doubt the old man's home. Jake thought, I'll bet that old-timer has imbibed enough whiskey to float a battleship. Jake knew he was going to go up before the officers returned and turn the old duffer loose. He glanced at Lige and figured his brother was thinking the same thing. Then Lige and Trudene started walking side by side toward home.

Jake felt Norma's arm around his waist, and when he looked at her, he sensed that her unease and tiredness were gone. He glanced around through the woodland. They were alone. Her face was flushed, and in her eyes was that darkening and reaching love that no man could mistake. He lifted her in his arms and began carrying her. He heard her soft laughter, and there was a growing tenderness for her, greater than he had ever known.